A Certain Grace

A Certain Grace

Stories by
Binnie Brennan

QUATTRO BOOKS

The publication of *A Certain Grace* has been generously supported by the Canada Council for the Arts and the Ontario Arts Council.

 Canada Council Conseil des Arts
for the Arts   du Canada

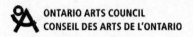 ONTARIO ARTS COUNCIL
CONSEIL DES ARTS DE L'ONTARIO

Cover design: Diane Mascherin
Cover image: Binnie Brennan
Author's photo: Kathy MacCulloch
Typography: Grey Wolf Typography
Editor: John Calabro

Library and Archives Canada Cataloguing in Publication

Brennan, Binnie
A certain grace / Binnie Brennan.

Issued also in electronic format.
ISBN 978-1-926802-84-8

I. Title.

PS8603.R461C47 2012   C813'.6   C2012-900352-2

Published by Quattro Books Inc.
89 Pinewood Avenue
Toronto, Ontario, M6C 2V2
www.quattrobooks.ca

Printed in Canada

For Tim,
Tamsyn and Avery

"Any story we remember is a truth about ourselves."

(From Helen Humphreys' poem, "Chinchilla"
Poetry collection: Anthem)

CONTENTS

How to Kill a Mannequin

LOUISE PINS THE LAST fold of blue silk to the headless dress-form, checks the floor for stray pins, and drapes her measuring tape across the dummy's shoulder, careful to avoid the amputation line marked by white stitches. Nearby, the blades of her scissors glint in the light. They, too, will need brushing off and putting in a safe place.

"Thank you very much," she whispers, not that she'd be heard over the clamour of the radio. Louise puts up with the country music the rest of the girls favour, as they hunch over their mannequins with pins clenched in their teeth, humming along. But how they can concentrate on their work is beyond her.

She looks out the window onto the busy street below. On such a day as this, with the sun high in the sky and the slightest breeze to cool her skin, Louise can't resist walking to the park. Surely she'll find a bench in a quiet corner where she can sit and eat her sandwich, perhaps even read her book undisturbed. Days like this one are made for exactly that, a small pocket of peace and quiet.

It's a superstition of hers to leave things just so, and to thank the mannequin, as she has read the medical students do the cadavers from which they learn. Every time Louise makes a dress, she imagines the personality that it will drape; it helps her to bring the fabric to life, make it into a thing of beauty. And so, with each new commission she re-names the dress-form. She hasn't yet thought of one for it this time around, but as the dress takes shape, the name will come.

Louise glances at the dressing mirror, pats her hair, and reaches in her purse for her lipstick. Squinting, she sees the ruddy-cheeked redhead of her youth. If she stands up straight and holds in her tummy, she nearly reaches the dress-form's shoulders.

"Be right back," she says in a low voice. After all, it would feel foolish if she let anyone overhear her talking to a mannequin.

The park is as Louise hoped, filled with people strolling around the pond, pushing baby carriages and sitting on benches, gathering rays of the elusive sun. It's been a cold, wet spring, but today's sun paints a thousand shades of green around her. Louise shuffles along the gravel path, admiring a rhododendron bush bursting with blossoms of a shade you'd think could only be produced in a plastics factory. A nearby wild rose sends its spicy perfume into the air, bringing Louise a childhood memory of climbing the rocks at Pebble Beach. A brief yearning grips her, and she stops for a moment with her eyes shut, thinking about rubber-toed sneakers, two-piece bathing suits, and the smell of a fresh Band-aid on her scraped knee.

A bus rumbles by, the Number Seven, which later today will take Louise home to her tidy apartment. She shakes a fleck of gravel from her sandal and continues on her way.

There is a vacant bench in the shade of a willow tree, facing the pond. She sits at one end and reaches into her purse for her sandwich, turkey breast and Cheez Whiz, with a papery slice of lettuce in the middle. After her first bite, Louise pulls out her book and removes the bookmark. She is near the end, a romance about a feisty middle-aged schoolteacher who finds herself on a remote island locking horns with a resident fisherman (widowed, his wife having drowned falling overboard during a storm) whose teenaged son refuses to stay in class. Already they've fought, kissed, argued, made love, and fought some more. Now the fisherman has enticed her on a dare to join him for a day on his fishing boat. If she can prove herself handy with a line, then he'll insist on his son going to school. When Louise finishes this one, she'll add it to the box of romances she'll eventually donate – anonymously, of course – to the church rummage sale.

As she turns the page, there is a thump and the bench joggles. A dreadlocked young man wearing a faded yellow shirt has hurled himself onto the far end, and is fiddling with his music gadget, from which wires travel to his ears. He turns and smiles, large, even teeth white against his dark skin and lively eyes creasing his cheeks. Louise smiles back. He isn't as young as she'd first thought.

"How's it goin' today, *madame*?" he asks.

"Just fine, thank you," Louise says. "Lovely day."

"It is indeed lovely," the man says in a booming voice. "Lovely, indeed – ha-ha!"

With that, he slaps his thighs in a calypso rhythm.

"My name is Badini, if you please," he says.

"Oh, Mr. Badini. How nice to meet you. I'm Louise." She looks at her sandwich, hungry, but not sure it would be polite to continue eating.

"Louise. My favourite auntie's name was Louise. It is a beautiful name. And please, it's just 'Badini'. No 'Mister'."

Badini's words carry a sing-song cadence in what, to Louise's ear, sounds almost like an Irish lilt, like Mr. O'Connor, who taught arithmetic at her high school. But she knows he isn't Irish; he must be from one of those Caribbean islands.

"Oh, thank you," she says, breathing a half-giggle. "Badini is a nice name, too. Where is it from?"

Badini points to his head, then his heart.

"It comes from in here, Louise, from right inside. It is mine alone. But you may use it."

Then he claps his hands, throws his head back and laughs in a rich and inviting bellow. Louise smiles at his gangly looseness, his easy smile. The freedom of choosing his own name. Badini is obviously a man to whom joy comes easily.

They have settled into a companionable silence, Louise reading her book and finishing her sandwich while Badini sits with his arms draped over the back of the bench. His eyes are half-closed and a beatific smile plays across his wide lips as his head nods in rhythm to whatever the ear buds are bringing him. It's peaceful in the park, just as Louise had hoped.

She closes her book and looks around. An elderly man makes his way gingerly, inching his walker along the footpath with a rhythmic scraping sound. The call of an angry duck grumbles from across the pond, and at the bench across from her, two young men hold hands and gaze into each other's eyes. One of them is wearing a plaid cap, and the other has on a shirt in the same plaid, blue shot with pink and yellow. Louise can't help noticing this; anything to do with fabric, she notices. Like the worn linen of Badini's shirt, a faded mustard colour that would look terrible on anyone else.

Louise opens her purse and reaches for her lipstick, but her attention is caught by an unexpected flash of light. She pulls out her scissors, with their long blades perfect for cutting bolts of cloth. She shakes her head – she must have put them in her purse by mistake before leaving the shop. She slips them back in and grabs the lipstick.

Louise sneaks another look at Badini, and lets her mind wander. What if she were the schoolteacher, and he the fisherman? Would they find the happy ending she knows is coming to the couple in her book, perhaps snuggled on the floorboards of his boat with the smell of fish to keep them company as they gaze at the stars above? Her face warms. She enjoys thinking these thoughts as much as she enjoys the smooth glide of pink lipstick.

A denim mini-skirt with long, tanned legs attached gets in the way of Louise's view of Badini as a young woman, staring intently at her phone, slowly turns and aims her tiny rear end at the space in the middle of the bench. Without taking her eyes from the screen, she sits down. Louise hardly feels the bench move. She adjusts her trousers and pulls her purse closer, and looks at the girl, whose lower lip hangs slightly in front of the upper, shiny with gloss. She is beautiful, with her streaked-blond hair tied back, and her eyes like slits hiding in a cloud of kohl. She is slim enough and stylish enough that she could be a model, or a mannequin in a store window. Louise thinks of the blue silk draped on the dress-form back at the shop, and in her mind's eye the dress begins to come to life, sleek and form-fitting and magical, befitting a prom queen.

The girl looks neither to the left nor the right, but suddenly frowns and punches the keypad with her thumb, and with a toss of her ponytail, whips the phone to her ear.

"'S'me. Crystal. Yeah, yeah," she says, her words uttered in a monotone staccato. "I dunno. No, yeah. No. Rully, she said no."

Louise has never understood how people don't seem to mind that the whole world can hear their half of a conversation, without being embarrassed. She hopes the girl will finish her call and move on, or better yet, move on and finish her call.

"Yeah, last night? We went out for steak sandwiches? And it was rully-rully good."

Louise allows a stab of irritation. She could certainly do without this intrusion – all she wanted was a quiet lunch at the park. She leans back and sneaks a look at Badini, who seems oblivious, his head nodding and his eyes still half-closed.

"Yeah. Yeah," the girl, Crystal, continues. "Then he bought me this jacket? And it was white with fringes? And it was rully-rully nice."

Louise clears her throat and stares at the girl, who gives her a cold glance and then studies her thumbnail.

"Then we went out? And he put away four beer? And he got rully-rully drunk."

At the other end of the bench, Badini's eyes have opened and he's watching the girl with interest. By now the blood is pounding in Louise's scalp. Crystal has ruined her lunch, her quiet time with that nice man. All that mundane and stupid yapping is sending her blood pressure through the roof. She glances at Badini, who shrugs and winks at her. Briefly her face warms at his wink, at their mutual understanding, but the moment passes and as the girl keeps droning into her telephone, Louise's fury spreads like a dirty fog. She sighs loudly and shakes her head. When the girl turns away from her, this time the bench does bounce with the deliberate force of it. Louise scowls and stares at her back – you can count the ribs beneath that skimpy tank top – but what's happening now? Badini is smiling. At the girl! And the girl is tossing her hair, flipping her ponytail in Louise's direction.

"I gotta go, 'bye." A pause, then, "That was my girlfriend? Melissa? She's rully-rully nice."

Badini's brilliant smile opens full-throttle and he holds out his hand.

"How's it goin' today, *mam'zelle*? My name is Badini, if you please."

Louise can practically hear the steel drums clanging off him, and his dreadlocks are probably filthy. Badini, my foot, she thinks – his name's probably David Smith. She yanks open her purse and throws in the lipstick. There is a satisfying ping of metal striking metal.

Louise glares at the ponytail. Looks down at the cutting scissors gleaming in her purse. She thinks of her nameless dress-form, drenched in blue silk, and wraps her fingers around the cold steel.

A While Ago

THE FINGERS OF HIS writing hand tingle as he picks up the Bic pen, a gift from his teacher once he stopped needing to use the pencil eraser so often. The clean page invites him, entices him with its pale blue lines, its pink margin. Marcus glances once at his new word, and adjusts the desk-lamp. Now that he has a desk in his own private bedroom, he can do his homework in peace-and-quiet.

There are two best things that ever happened, and they both happened just before his twenty-sixth birthday: one was his own bedroom, all to himself. And the other was his dictionary, a gift from the counselors at the group home. "Happy Birthday to our favourite reader 'n writer," the birthday card said. Lindsay told him that *'n* is the lazy way of writing *and*.

Marcus looks again at his new word.

Ago: *adv.* earlier; before the present.

The Oxford English Dictionary is his good friend; it always tells him clearly what he needs to know about a word. Marcus smiles as he adds "ago" to his word list. A-G-O, a purple-black word. *Adv*, that means adverb, Mr. Phillips told him so. But how is "ago" an adverb? Doesn't an adverb mod – mid – no, modify a verb? He will have to check with Mr. Phillips tomorrow morning at school. Meanwhile he prints "ago" and its definition with great care, adding another triumph to his list.

Soon the words stare back at him, dark blue letters held in place by the pale blue lines and the pink margin, glowing from the white page in his notebook. Marcus loves to look at his word list. He loves to print, to build words from the first letter to the last. Nothing makes him happier than to see a word come out of the lines and curves from the tip of his ball-point pen. Bic, it says on it, but really it should have a silent k, just like "brick."

Marcus remembers the first time he figured out a silent-letter word. At first he thought it was "shoulder," but there weren't enough syllables, so for a while he was confused. He stared and stared at the letters on the green flash card, upper-case, strong and black. For a long time the letters stared back at him. Then they started to move, the way they do just before they mean something. The letters moved in slow waves, then faster, and then they twitched. Marcus sucked in his breath and opened his eyes wide.

"Should," he shouted, and jumped up from his chair, sending it tumbling back with a clatter. Mr. Phillips high-fived him so hard his hand hurt, but Marcus didn't mind. His face hurt even more, he smiled and laughed so much. To celebrate, Mr. Phillips bought them both a coffee at Tim Hortons, a medium black for himself and a large double-double for Marcus. His favourite.

That was a long time ago. At least, Marcus thinks it was. Or maybe it was just a while ago.

Ago: *adv,* earlier; before the present.

A long time ago seems so far away. Marcus writes the words down underneath his definition, which will please Mr. Phillips. "It's a good way to round out your list," he always says. "That way the word will belong to you." Marcus loves it when a new word belongs to him. Not many things do, so when, for example, "adventure" joined his list, with its own sentence attached, he flapped his arms and clapped, he was so proud and so happy. "Reading is its own adventure," he had written. Just like Mr. Phillips likes to say every time they start a new book together. And it is; he knows that. Just last week, he and Mr. Phillips finished reading *Charlie and the Chocolate Factory*, by Mr. Roald Dahl. Now, there's an adventure. At night, when the lights are out in the group home and the yellow street light cuts the dark through his window, Marcus lies in bed and thinks about the chocolate river, the square candies that look round (which is another way of saying they look around at things), and how hungry and poor Charlie Bucket was. And he thinks about how smart Mr. Roald Dahl was to have written that book. Mr. Phillips says he wrote it many years ago, and it must have been, because first he had to type it, and then someone made the pictures, and then someone else made the books. And that all takes time.

Many years ago.

Ago. It's a happy-sad word, Marcus thinks. A while ago he learned how to read, how to print. Many years ago, Mr. Roald Dahl wrote his book. And some time ago, Mr. Phillips became his teacher, his hero. Three happy things.

A long time ago, now that's different altogether.

A long time ago he lived in a car with Rambo. Rambo was his only friend, but he was often angry, and sometimes he tied an old sock around his arm and turned his back on him. Marcus felt bad every time, and while Rambo was busy taking his medicine, Marcus told him over and over again that he was sorry. By the time he untied his sock and turned around again, Rambo would be smiling, and then he'd close his eyes and sleep awhile. It was always a relief knowing Rambo was still his friend.

An even longer time ago there was the hospital, but thinking about that fills the back of Marcus' nose with nasty-sick smells that make his legs feel like running.

But the longest time ago there was his Uncle Lou, whose face turned purple every time he had to straighten Marcus out. "Boy, don't make me have to straighten you out," he'd yell before coming after him. Marcus doesn't remember why he'd needed straightening out, and he doesn't remember much about Uncle Lou's house, except sometimes he slept in the closet at night, lying on a coat so his behind wouldn't be so sore. The old coat scratched his face and smelled sour, and there was too much dog hair on the floor, and Marcus worried he might sneeze and give himself away. One time he half woke up, and while he tried to sort out what was happening, Uncle Lou laid him down on his bed and tucked him in. His eyes were red and watery, and when he looked away and wiped his nose on the back of his blue sleeve, Marcus felt sick and worried. Confused. So he closed his eyes hard until the orange and blue spots appeared, and when Uncle Lou's feet shuffled out to the hallway, Marcus pulled the blanket over his head. He felt safer that way.

Three sad things. Marcus prefers a while ago, so he crosses out "a long time" and underneath he writes "a while." He hopes Mr. Phillips won't mind.

Marcus looks at the page. It no longer glows, but is dulled by the crossing-out. He forgot he was using his pen, and you can't erase ink. It's ruined, he knows it, and he wishes the banging in his ears would stop. Now he has to do it all over again. What if Mr. Phillips takes away his new pen? He stands, then sits, puts his hands over his face, and rocks back and forth. Breathes twice loudly, pounds himself with his fists. Closes his eyes and starts to count. By the time he reaches twenty-eight, his favourite number, his face is no longer too tight and he is fine. Marcus breathes deeply and looks at the page again. It's not so bad, and maybe Mr. Phillips will let him paint over the mistake with liquid paper. That will fix it right up, and he can write it again. "A while ago." The paper looks brighter already. Tomorrow the mistake will have happened a while ago.

Marcus will add three more words to his list. He reads the next two in the dictionary: *Agog*, then *agogic*. Lots of lovely "g's," which are fancy letters, all curls and purple-black swirls. Beyond, he sees *a gogo*, still more "g's" but mostly black. He will add the three new words to his list, then get ready for bed. At least, he thought he would, but now he can't. It's raining.

Marcus sighs, puts his pen in his pencil case, and zips it closed. He closes his notebook and places it on the bureau next to where his folded-up underpants and his undershirt sit waiting for him to put them on in the morning. Then he pulls back the sheet and climbs into bed, and pulls the chain on the lamp. Against the darkness, Marcus squeezes his eyes shut, and begins to count the raindrops. Orange and blue spots spray before his closed eyes. He hopes the rain will continue to fall slowly, at least until his eyelids soften and he goes to sleep. The faster the rain comes down, the harder it is to count.

The trouble with rain is that sometimes there's thunder. And when there's thunder, there's usually lightning. And the trouble with lightning is that it scares Marcus witless, just like Rambo used to say whenever the gangs came around with knives hidden under their socks. "C'mon man, let's go.

These guys scare me witless." Really he meant shitless, but Rambo had his polite side, and he liked to say things the nice way, especially since Marcus asked him to. *There's no call for profanity*, he once said, just like the nice lady at the soup kitchen once told the man in front of him. Rambo had stared at him with his blue-red eyes and his almost toothless mouth hanging open, and Marcus worried for a minute that he'd made him mad again. Then the black O of Rambo's mouth turned into a pink banana, and rare crinkles appeared on his cheeks and around his eyes, and he started to laugh. "You're a truckin' piece of work, man," he bellowed, reaching across and thumping Marcus on the shoulder, the way the football players do on TV. The top of Marcus' head tingled, he was so happy and relieved, and from then on Rambo said things like "witless," and "truck" for that other bad word.

But lightning is a worry. When thunder bangs like the world's biggest kitchen pots slamming together, Marcus dreads the coming flash of light. It reminds him of something awful, he's not sure what, but it always leaves him shaking and sweating, and his head hurts afterwards.

He will count, this time he will count, just like Mr. Phillips told him to. Then he will know how far away the storm is, and maybe it won't be quite as scary as the last time. Already he's lost track of the raindrops, which upsets him, although not as much as the prospect of lightning does. This time he gets as far as fourteen thousand, three hundred-twenty-two. Which is three thousand, four hundred-forty-seven more than the last time it rained, and that's a comfort.

Marcus pulls the blanket over his head, and waits for the thunder. When finally he opens his eyes to the wet-smelling, green-and-yellow morning, he realizes the thunder never did come.

The morning starts badly, and Marcus just knows the whole day will be off. He feels worried and unsteady. Everything was fine until Jimmy-next-door spilled his orange juice.

It's one thing if Marcus spills something; he just holds his breath, and when he's certain nobody's going to straighten him out, he takes the cloth handed to him by one of the counselors and wipes it up. But when Jimmy-next-door spills his juice, he gets mad, and when he's mad he's noisy. Like this morning, he yelled a lot, not real words, but noises like *Ooooaaffaaalo*, and *Ack-ack-ack*. Then Michael and Lindsay, the two counselors here for breakfast, tried to help. Michael stood behind Jimmy and put his arms around him, and Lindsay spoke to him in her soft-soft voice, saying things like, "It's okay, Jim, you don't need to be angry. Watch me clean it up, it's easy. Just like this." And just like that, Lindsay cleaned it up.

After that, Michael talked to Jimmy about the ball game, and then he reminded him about morning quiet. Sure, it was quiet in the kitchen again, but the air was noisy, and Marcus wished Jimmy-next-door had never spilled his juice. Dan didn't even finish his toast. Instead, he picked up his rubber band and went over by the window. Marcus didn't like to see him do it, but Dan stood there and rocked back and forth and went flick-flick-flick with his rubber band around his wrist, and every time he flicked, Marcus knew it stung him. Sal and Marcus stayed in their seats, and Sal said, "Mind if I eat your toast?" Which was nice, because he doesn't usually ask. Marcus figured Sal must have felt bad about the noise in the air. Jimmy breathed hard a few times, then Lindsay poured him a new cup of juice and sat down and helped him drink it slower. That's the thing with Jimmy-next-door, he does things too fast. And then he gets noisy.

Sometimes at night, when the orange and blue spots have faded and Marcus' eyelids are soft and his mouth falls open, he is frightened awake by Jimmy's pounding on the wall. It usually takes a while for his heart to stop thumping, but Marcus has learned to count the thumps backwards from a hundred and go back to sleep.

Marcus is glad he's in the same taxi as Sal and Michael. Sal likes to sit up front with Ralph-the-driver, which means Michael is in the back seat with Marcus. While Sal helps the driver put the key in the hole, the two of them play the license-plate game, which is great. One time Marcus saw a license plate that was shaped like a polar bear. Michael told him it was from the Yukon, which is far away and has a lot of snow. Mr. Phillips showed him where it is on the map, and told him that in the Yukon, at night when it's really, really cold, the sky turns all kinds of colours, like green and yellow and pink, and that's called the *aurora borealis*. Marcus added it to his list. He liked the shape of the words, their own colours, green-yellow-pink but also purple. But he's not sure he'd want to see the aurora borealis for real. He likes his night sky dark.

"Try and sit still, buddy." Michael's hand is warm on his shoulder. Marcus stops rocking, but only long enough to open the ash-tray in back of Ralph-the-driver's seat. The dried-up circle of gum is still there from the last time, and the time before, and the time before that. Marcus tries but he can't remember when he first noticed the pink circle of gum in the ash-tray. Maybe it's been there forever. He stops thinking about the gum, and starts to rock again.

It's hard to sit still before school, especially when he's got new words to show Mr. Phillips. Michael points to a license plate attached to a red car. Marcus freezes and squints. The blue-and-white numbers and letters are rounder and farther apart than the Yukon license plate numbers and letters. The province's name begins and ends with 'O.' The letters move fast and then faster than the car, blue-black, then they twitch. "Ontario," Marcus shouts, and Michael gives him a high-five.

The noise is quick and awful, kind of a thud and a crack, the way it might sound if you dropped a boulder on top of another boulder. It seems a long time between when Marcus' head hits the back of the seat, then is thrown forward. The seatbelt strap grabs him hard across the chest, and his hand, still in flight from the high-five, slams into the back of the driver's seat, right against the opened ash-tray. Marcus is aware that two other hands have shot out, one to save him and one to save Sal.

"Shit," someone says in a loud voice. "Everyone all right?" Marcus is too busy trying to breathe to say anything about profanity.

"You okay, buddy?" Michael reaches for his high-five hand, which is red with blood but doesn't hurt.

"It doesn't hurt, doesn't hurt," he says in a voice that sounds like someone else's. The words trip over his breath, which keeps getting stuck. Sal's head is bent forward, and his shoulders are going up and down.

"It's okay, buddy, breathe slowly. Slowly, okay? Sal, you all right? Ralph? Everyone okay?"

Ralph-the-driver is fine, but he's mad at the driver behind them. He takes the key out of the hole and lets Sal hold it, then he gets out of the taxi. Right away Sal's shoulders stop going up and down, and he stares at the key with his red eyes and his nose running. Marcus turns around to see what Ralph-the-driver is doing, and wonders if there will be a fist fight. He hopes not.

A long time ago, when he and Rambo lived in the car together, someone tried to break into the trunk while they were sleeping. The man was wearing a ball cap pulled down low, so Marcus couldn't see his face when Rambo went after him. But he could see Rambo's face, which was red and veiny, as he lay on the ground and the man punched him and punched him. Then the ball-capped man grabbed some stuff out of the trunk and ran away. Marcus helped Rambo to his feet, and for some reason he was the only one crying as he offered Rambo his sleeve to wipe his bleeding nose.

Ralph-the-driver is standing next to a small woman whose eyes are big and scared. The two of them look at the back of the taxi and point. Ralph pulls a small notebook from his shirt pocket, and Marcus wonders if he's got a new word. But the woman hands him a piece of paper, and he copies some of her words in his notebook.

"Nothing serious," says Ralph-the-driver when he climbs back into the taxi. "How is everyone?"

"I think we should get Marcus to a doctor," Michael says. Marcus doesn't know why, although his hand is now wrapped in Michael's handkerchief, which is blue like the sky. There is a dark red shape against the blue, and it is growing. Marcus thinks of the polar bear license plate, of Mr. Phillips' map of the Yukon, and he closes his eyes and shivers.

His hand aches. The bandage glows, as white as a fresh page in his notebook, although the pink margin line is hiding under the bandage, held together by four stitches. The doctor was nice, and told Marcus how strong and brave he was while he got his hand ready for the stitches. "Just a little freezing," he said, but Marcus knew by the way Michael looked at him and then looked away from him that it would be bad. And it was. Michael sat behind him and wrapped his arms around him in a big hug, and the nurse who smelled like flowers held down his arm while the doctor put in the freezing. But there was nothing cold about the freezing; in fact, it burned more than the cigarette butt Uncle Lou once held against his leg. Marcus screamed and cried, and Michael said over and over again how sorry he was, and that it'd be all done in a minute. So they counted together, and he was right, the freezing-burning was done in a minute. Less, in fact. More like twenty-two seconds.

When the doctor was finished with the stitches, he shook Marcus' other hand, which made him feel important. And the nurse smiled in a pretty way and handed him his own pair of doctor gloves to take home with him. She said he deserved them.

Marcus looks at the pill bottle Lindsay is holding, the one she reached for when he told her his hand was sore.

"The doctor said you're to have two of these every four hours, Marcus." She fills the green plastic cup, Marcus' favourite, with water, and hands him the pills. "It'll help stop the pain." Lindsay puts the bottle back in the cabinet and locks it with the key she's got attached to the yellow plastic coil on her wrist, but not before Marcus has seen the letters. Another "A" word for his list. A-D-V-I-L, he puts in his memory, for later, when he goes to his room and opens his notebook. Already Marcus knows what the sentence will say: "Advil helps stop the pain." He will copy the words down from his own memory, not from the dictionary, and Mr. Phillips will think that's great. Maybe he'll even buy him a large coffee, a double-double, from Tim Hortons.

The hand he holds the pen with is the hand that's sore and bandaged. Marcus thinks about how, just a while ago, it wasn't sore, and he could hold his new Bic pen and write down words like Advil. But now it's sore and there's a big white bandage, and he can't write anything. The thought saddens him, and the air around him goes heavy, but only for a moment. Then the fingers of his other hand tingle, and he knows everything will be all right.

Her Private Sorrow

SHE REMEMBERS LARGE THINGS and small: leaves blinking gold and scarlet in the light of the low-lying sun; the scent of her daughter's head, talcum-powder wisps of auburn soft against her cheek as the baby leaned toward her coming childhood. Her grandfather's massive hands, as vivid to her now as they were forty years ago, horned nails and folds of mottled skin through which the strength of his youth revealed itself: hands that once cradled her, chopped down trees, pulled on the tiller, and grasped the bayonet that both took lives and saved his own. Buppa's hands.

What does any of it tell her? Her daughter, now grown and restless, travels the globe saving souls and breaking hearts. Buppa's ashes rest in the ground near his favourite harbour, where, for the last fifteen years, every year Addie lays her poppy.

Herbert "Buppa" Strong

November 11, 1904 – March 7, 1996

Much loved and deeply missed

Only the leaves remain true to their destiny, flashing red-gold in the early winter light.

Addie pulls the door closed behind her, shutting out the November cold. She takes off her gloves – thank God for rabbit fur, no matter what Emily has to say about the butchering of innocent animals, which is easy enough for her to proclaim from her pedestal in Delhi, or is it Mumbai this month? Some place warm. Addie has endured forty-nine Canadian winters. It took until recently for her to admit that fur equals warm, which equals tolerable living for five months of the year. She will not be cold.

So she lays the fur-lined gloves across the radiator, also her hat. The coat she drapes over a chair, rather than leaving it to freeze on the storm-porch.

The telephone is flashing with messages. On her way to it, Addie presses the start button and the computer wheezes to life. A glass of wine would suit her just now, but all the fridge will yield is a dribble of juice. It's about time she bought some groceries, real groceries, not just the ninety-nine cent frozen dinners she's been eating. She envisions steaming vats of soup, home-made cornbread, a pot of vegetarian chili. Winter food stored in yogurt containers, tucked away in the freezer before Emily comes home for Christmas. If she comes home.

The telephone winks, come-hither. Addie relents.

"This is Canadian Consumers calling to see if you'd be interested..."

She beeps it away into oblivion. Next, a reminder from the library in a creepy, mechanical voice that her books are overdue. Tonight she must finish reading Vassanji's travel memoir on India. She's been hoping for some insight to her daughter's fascination with the place, but so far she doesn't see it. The history, the crowds, the poverty; she finds the thought of it all overwhelming, oppressive.

There is another reminder, from the dentist, about Friday's cleaning.

Then: *"Mum? Mum, it's me, Emmie…"*

Addie straightens, holds her breath. Emily hasn't let her use her baby name in years. Something's wrong.

"I'm just calling to tell you I miss you, Mum. That, and…"

What? And what? Addie turns around and stares through the window as though the answer might lie outside in the dark.

"…and I hope everything's all right. I dunno, I just wanted to hear your voice, it being Remembrance Day and all. Oh well, at least I got your voice mail. I'll have Internet soon – I'm moving on from Mumbai in a day or two, heading south. Love you, Mum. Miss you. Buppa, too."

The telephone hums her daughter's absence. Remembrance Day, of course. Addie releases her breath slowly. Emily is a softie at heart. She has remembered that today is Buppa's birthday.

The first few years after his death, Emily demanded a cake on his birthdays, and left a piece for him at his place at the kitchen table with a card signed "Buppa's Little Emmie," his nickname for her. The first time she discovered it uneaten, she was inconsolable.

Cake or no cake, sixteen years later, no matter where she is in the world, she is still Buppa's Little Emmie. Addie's face softens in a smile.

There remains one message. *Later*, Addie thinks. She needs to absorb her daughter's words, listen to them again to bring her closer. In spite of the great distance between them, or maybe because of it, Addie imagines a closeness.

Love you, Mum echoes in her mind as she returns the flashing telephone to its cradle, words she can never, ever say with such ease.

There is comfort in nostalgia, even though the memories can bring with them great pain. So Addie thinks as she stops at the doorway to Emily's bedroom.

"We are what we repeatedly do. Excellence, then, is not an act but a habit," proclaims Aristotle on a hand-printed sign pinned to the wall over the desk.

"The toughest thing about being a success is that you've got to keep on being a success," according to Irving Berlin.

Ghandi stares down at her from the wall above the bed, his eyes sweet and knowing behind wire rims: "Be the change you want to see in the world."

For all the posters and motivational quotations pinned to the wall, it is the bookshelf that reveals the most about her daughter. Tucked between *The Hobbit* and *The Wind in the Willows* there is a battered copy of *The Diary of Anne Frank*. Farther along the shelf, a collection of sports magazines – hockey, skateboarding, and horseback riding. An old wrist cast, scuffed and covered in signatures, holds within it Emily's rolled-up high school diploma. On the top shelf there is a collection of Charlie Brown books, Addie's own, scavenged from Buppa's attic when she finally sold the family home. Emily's enchantment with the Peanuts gang came from her need to see Charlie Brown finally succeed at kicking the football and flying his kite, winning an argument with Lucy. That he never did so only served to broaden Emily's compassion for some and disdain for others. *Lord of the Flies*, appropriately, sits dog-eared next to the Charlie Brown collection. Poor Piggy with his broken glasses.

And now Emily is in India, tending to the orphans, moving from one state of impoverishment to another. She, herself, an orphan of sorts.

Addie steps back into the hallway and moves on to her own bedroom, her sanctuary, and switches on the light. She spends a moment standing at the doorway, gazing around the room. It is just as she likes it, tidy with white walls and bedding, her grandmother's dresser tall by the window, and the family rocking chair draped in a translucent lace shawl, stitches rendered perfectly by Grammy's hands.

There is not a thing out of place. A silver-framed photograph of six-year-old Emily beaming up at Buppa sits on the dresser. She is pigtailed and missing a front tooth, a far cry from the willowy, dreadlocked young woman now backpacking around India. "She keeps me young," Buppa used to say, and this is how Addie chooses to remember him, restored in his old age by the thrill of his great-grandchild.

They had one more year of him, nearly to the day. And then, a few weeks before Emily's seventh birthday, he was gone. *Much loved and deeply missed.* Addie chose the words for his grave stone; has run her fingertips along the engraving countless times.

She closes her eyes, breathes deeply, and opens them again.

An orchid, perfect in its pale, inquiring reach, saves the room from austerity, placed on the bedside-table next to Buppa's wind-up alarm clock that ticks its steady beat, a reminder that the day has passed into night. Behind the clock the telephone is flashing the last message, the one she didn't take.

Addie sits on the edge of the bed and pulls off her socks, reaches with cold toes for her slippers. Absently she picks up the telephone and pokes in the code.

"Addie? Uh... hi, this is Frank."

She frowns. Who is Frank? Does she even know a Frank? Whoever he is, he sounds nervous, unsure. Frank clears his throat.

"Yeah, it's Frank, here. I'm, um, I'm Susan's brother. Susan, you know, Darren's wife. I'm her brother. That Frank."

Addie straightens. *That* Frank: Darren's brother-in-law, the pediatrician. Why on earth is her ex-husband's brother-in-law leaving her a message?

"Listen, uh, bad news. Susan asked me to call you and let you know that, um, Darren suffered a stroke today. He's not... he's probably not going to make it through the night."

Frank is a doctor, everything should be all right. Addie grasps at reason before the truth of his words sets in and her heart begins to pound.

He's probably not going to make it through the night.

"Sorry to leave a message like this, Addie, but I thought you should know. I'll call you when..." Frank clears his throat. "I'll call if there's any change."

She glances at the photo on the dresser, willing her accelerating heart to slow. Buppa is looking straight at the camera, his bristly eyebrows arched in delight as he listens to what his great-granddaughter is telling him.

They were so close, those two, one always near the other, Buppa revelling in Emmie's observations and Emmie frowning, then nodding at his. They possessed endless room in their hearts for each other.

The hand holding the phone begins to tremble. She must find her daughter, Darren's baby girl. And then she must tell her that her father is dying, that he may already be dead. The telephone rattles against the table as she sets it down beside the clock.

Later, much later, after the next call from Frank, the one that tells her the inevitable has happened, Addie wakens. The backs of her legs burn, ready for flight, and her breathing is ragged. A dream has wrenched her here, an old enemy she has tried for years to keep at bay: through rainforest-dappled light Addie stares at a swinging bridge over a deep chasm. Emily's small red sneaker, with its rubber toe pointing away from her, sits by the edge of a broken board. Emily is gone and Addie cannot find her, not ever.

The first time she dreamed this was during the custody trial. Even after she emerged from that hideous day, the victory sitting like a stone in her mouth as she tried to erase the memory of Darren's bald scalp reddening, the choking sound from the back of his throat as they both realized she, Addie, was deemed the better parent – even then the dream came to her. What a relief when Emily outgrew the little red sneakers, and with the simplicity of childhood fickleness her favourite colour changed from red to green, and a few months later, in time for still larger shoes, blue.

But still the dream came.

Addie has known always that she could never keep for her own what she loved the most. She has no memory of being struck by this notion, so much as having it settle on her like a layer of dust as she realized she was the only girl at her school living with her grandparents.

How come your dad looks so old?

Why aren't you making a Mother's Day card like everyone else?

Before her memory began, her own parents died in a ditch, the horn blaring and tires still spinning. She cannot remember who they were; only that they weren't.

She stands at the back, off to one side, watching as the pews fill. Footsteps and hushed voices chase around the dark, stone walls, and the stained-glass windows hold a dull glow.

Most of the faces are strange to her, men in suits and ties, women wearing hose and heels. Lipstick. They remind her of her friends' parents when she was in Sunday School, grownups with two cars in the driveway, two-point-two kids, and avocado-coloured appliances in their kitchens. This is now her generation, and they are even a little older than the parents of her recollection. Addie looks at the backs of tidy, coiffed heads and doesn't feel so grown-up.

There have been a few familiar faces, friends from before the divorce. Friends whose loyalty remained with Darren. He may have lost parental custody, but he won full custody of their social life. *She* had left him; *she* had been the one to drift out of love. *How could she?* Darren was kind and funny and reliable, and he really did love her. If he couldn't understand why she'd left, neither could their friends.

Addie ponders the so-called healing properties of time. Over the years the pain and permanence of those losses have smoothed, if not vanished entirely. Addie can't begrudge her former friends. She only hopes she needn't speak to them – not here, not now.

The church fills with the reedy sound of the organ as it wheezes out a dirge-like rendering of something familiar and sad.

Addie takes a seat in the last pew, on the aisle near the door. She thinks back to the last time she saw Darren, the last words he'd spoken to her, delivered at Emily's going-away party only two short months ago.

"It would have been nice to know about this – all of this – a little in advance," Darren had said in a low voice, but not too low as to be lost under the thud-thud of the music playing in the living room. Addie's jaw had clenched, then unclenched, her back molars grinding. Three of Emily's friends bustled giggling into the kitchen as she pointed the wine bottle at his glass.

"No, thanks." Darren placed his empty glass on the counter and looked at the floor while the girls opened and closed cupboards.

"Everyone having fun?" Addie said, forcing a smile.

"Great party, Miz Strong," one of the girls said, flicking her ponytail over her shoulder. "I bet you'll miss Emily, though."

"Yes, it'll be quiet around here. Are you looking for glasses?"

"S'okay, Taylor's got them."

The girls crowded back into the living room. As the door swung open, laughter erupted; the music grew louder.

"Why didn't you let me know sooner that she's leaving? For chrissakes, India? For a whole year?"

His reddening forehead shone a warning. Once upon a time, Addie called it his mood ring. Now she had to look away from it and calm her own flaming pulse that was threatening to pound its way to a migraine headache.

"Darren, she's twenty-two years old. I'd have thought she'd tell you herself."

"Yeah, well, she didn't." Darren picked up his wine glass and held it out. "I'll have some, after all. Why India, anyway?"

"Frankly, I don't know what the appeal is." Addie poured the last of the bottle into his glass. "But she's got it in her head that she's going to help out at an orphanage, and you know as well as I do, there's no more stopping Emily than a runaway train."

"I have a job for her at the office any time she wants it. She knows that."

"That's great, Darren, but Emily's not exactly an office type. *You* know *that*, right?" The thought of their restless, dreadlocked daughter sitting at a computer screen for eight hours a day forced a cold smile to Addie's face.

"Not funny, Addie. Of course I do, I'm her father."

She opened her mouth to speak, thought the better of it, and reached into the fridge for another bottle. Again, her molars ground against each other.

"It's just that…" The look on Darren's face was complicated. "Aren't you the least bit worried about her?"

Addie blinked. "Worried? Of course I'm worried," she said. "But Emily's a big girl; she'll be able to take care of herself. Besides, she's hooking up to the orphanage once she arrives. It's an international program. She'll be fine. Think of the growing up she'll do." She paused and gulped the dregs from her glass while Darren stood rigid with his arms crossed, glaring at her. "Oh, for God's sake," she said, "Darren, let it go."

The stare Darren fixed on her left her feeling disconcerted, as though *she'd* missed the point to something. Addie took a deep breath and swallowed back an old irritation, her head pounding in rhythm to the music blaring in the other room.

"I'll put some money in her account first thing in the morning," Darren said, draining his glass. "Nice party. Thanks for the invitation." He tipped the empty glass in her direction and pushed his way through the swinging door. Addie's jaw was beginning to ache, her head throbbing. His sarcasm was not lost on her.

Darren paused in the doorway and turned. "You could have told me."

The door squeaked, then squeaked again as it swung shut and settled. Addie let out a slow, measured breath.

There was a break in the music through which Emily's voice reached her.

"Bye, Daddy! I'll text you when I get there. Love you."

Addie turned on the faucet and scrubbed her wine glass. She didn't need to hear his reply.

The congregation rises for the arrival of Darren's family. *The Lord giveth and the Lord taketh away…* The minister intones about a man he never knew, but who attended services twice a year and had his children baptized as insurance, both his first daughter and then his second batch. Emily Strong O'Donnell, Addie recalls, the triumph of Buppa's name – Strong, like his hands – one of the earliest cracks in her marriage, one of a thousand negotiations that started in the bedroom and wound up in a courtroom nine years later.

The newly-widowed Susan is flanked by her brothers, Frank and John. Her head is bowed, her hand to her mouth as she takes quick steps down the aisle, narrow ankles held up by impossibly high heels. Behind her follow the girls, whose names Addie struggles for in vain. Skinny, pale girls not yet grown into their teeth, gangly and sad; neither of them holds a glimmer of Emily, despite their shared genes. Frank's eyes find her and he nods, almost a signal, as though Addie should now take her leave.

It is a strange and lonely grief, that of the ex-wife of the deceased, one that exhausts her. She shrugs on her coat and is reaching for her purse when a nasal voice reaches her.

"Addie? Addie, is that you?"

It's Judith-Ann, one of the many who remained in Darren's circle. She is gaunt, the girlish blue eyes of her youth now set deep in her face, rendering her nose pointy. Perfectly-behaved bangs hang straight down her forehead, covering the eyebrows that are now surely raised in surprise at seeing her here.

"Judith-Ann, hi. I was just leaving…"

"Oh, Addie. This must be… well, so hard for you."

"Yes, it's sad, especially for Emily, who can't…"

"Oh, Emily!" Judith-Ann cries, anguish pulling the skin taut across her nose. "Where is she? How is she?"

"Em's in India, somewhere in the South. She's…"

"Can you believe how old our babies are? I mean, really! Zachary's twenty-two, so that means Emily's…"

"Also twenty-two." Addie finishes the thought, pushing aside memories of their shared pregnancies, the breastfeeding meetings Judith-Ann dragged her to, even though Addie was perfectly happy to feed the baby from a bottle. "What's Zachary up to?"

She does not wish to talk; asking is the best alternative. She pretends to listen as Judith-Ann gushes about Zachary's successes and those of his younger sisters, a home-schooled brood of overachievers, all of them virtuoso violin or piano players doing double majors in theatre studies and neuroscience. Or something. Judith-Ann's words have a careful, practiced cadence to them, as though well-used.

"I really must go," Addie says firmly, once there is a break in Judith-Ann's soliloquy. Addie is near boiling point, and she cannot stand to be in this church for one more second. She has no real place in Darren's death, nowhere to take her own, private sorrow other than to go home and try once again to find Emily.

When Emily brought home her first boyfriend, Addie felt nothing but revulsion. The thought of her daughter being touched by this young, feral-looking boy in ripped jeans and with pierced eyebrows set off her gag reflex. It wasn't so much a maternal jolt as simple disgust. But she put up with it, even sanctioned by her silence the boy's staying over, silence which Emily took for permission.

A few months later, Addie held her sobbing daughter's hand in the waiting room and stared ahead at the painting on the wall, bold, ugly strokes depicting a sailboat on the harbour. After the abortion, she went through the motions of buckling Emily's seatbelt, handing her tissues, and later that night, tucking her into bed as she had when she was a little girl.

"You're the best mother in the world," Emily wept, flinging her arms around Addie in a rare embrace.

But she wasn't. Addie knew it then and she knows it now. All she felt, all she *could* feel of her daughter's pain was her own numbness, the familiar distance sliding her safely aside from the daughter she loved. But it was the end of the feral-looking boyfriend, and there was much to be said for that.

There is a shoebox filled with old photos nestled on a high shelf in Emily's bedroom closet. Addie pushes aside a scuffed pair of Birkenstocks, left there for Emily's rare visits home, and teases the shoebox forward with her fingers. It tips into her outstretched hands, the shift in gravity pushing the box's contents to the front with a shuffle and a clunk. It is heavier than Addie remembers.

She sits on Emily's bed and gives the lid a puff before lifting it. Dust particles shoot into the air and hang suspended and glittering in a sunbeam from the window.

Addie opens the box, flips through the contents. Tries not to think too hard about the little girl beneath her hands, the sad days and the good ones, the fatigue of raising her alone.

Suddenly it is there, still in its cardboard frame.

In the photograph stands Buppa, his blue eyes pale against the sepia. A young man of eighteen, stiff in his Sunday jacket, his hair sleekened with oil, a black band around his arm. Before him sits his mother, with her stern face tightened by grief and her pulled-back hair. To her left sits Buppa's father, his prominent nose framed by mutton chops and a waxed moustache, his head seemingly held in place by the high, starched collar and cravat. Neither man nor wife touches the other.

On either side and before the parents stand the rest of the surviving siblings, Great-Aunt Rita small but poised, her hair brushed to a sheen and held in place by a discreet black ribbon, her lips pursed and eyes looking straight at the camera. The twins, Chester and Belinda, flank their older sister, four bewildered eyes and two pouting mouths, still young enough that Chester sports knee pants and a tumble of ringlets.

It might have been just another family portrait, but for the shades of black ribbon and sadness, the tilt of a head, the frozen, forced look of not-quite-breathing in the mother, a look Addie has seen in her own mirror a hundred times. Each family member holds something small – a doll, a handkerchief, a Bible. A dried posie. A Japanese fan folded shut in Mother's hand. Favourite belongings of the sister now gone, taken from them by pneumonia.

You can almost hear the minister intone the words of little comfort: *Christ is risen*, but not Buppa's dear sister, not his beloved Adele, with whom he once ran in the lupin fields behind the barn, shouting and laughing and brushing ants off the ginger snaps Adele had nicked from the pantry as they cooled.

Somewhere in the kitchen, tucked in a cookbook Addie never uses, is a yellowed index card, written in the tell-tale slant of her grandmother's hand, the family ginger snap recipe. Addie remembers the spiced crunch, the need for a glass of milk to soften the hard, brown rectangle. As a child she much preferred her cookies storebought, bland and overly-sweet. Now she craves the bite of ginger, the underlying hum of clove and molasses stirred and rolled with patience and a sure hand, and then chilled in the icebox before being sliced and baked. Cooled in the pantry.

They knew how to grieve, those blank-eyed ancestors of hers. Addie envies them their certainty, the comfort of their ritual. A daughter dies. You lay her out pale as snow in the parlour, and then you bury her to the droning of the minister, the wheezing of the church organ. You wear a black ribbon on your sleeve or in your hair, and you hold her favourite hanky for a family portrait of grief, something strangers can look at years from now and pause over. Then you give someone else the dead one's name to honour her life, to try to hang on to her for a while longer.

When your ex-husband dies, there is no such ritual and little comfort.

She holds the photograph beside the one of Buppa and Emily. Tomorrow she'll buy a frame for it, give it a place of prominence. For now, the weight of fatigue presses against her. Addie looks longingly at the soft, white pillows, her grandmother's shawl. The clock ticks, and beside it the telephone blinks, slightly behind the clock's tempo.

Addie lifts the phone from its cradle and punches in the code.

"Mum? You'll never guess what I did last night!"

Emily's voice sounds far too happy for a girl whose father has just been buried. Addie shakes her head, as though ridding herself of another foolish thought. Emmie still does not know, she reminds herself.

"It was so awesome, I delivered a baby! A slippery, beautiful baby with guck all over it. It was just so amazing, so beautiful, Mum. I wish…"

Emily's voice catches, and she makes a small inhaling sound. Addie holds her breath, thinking of her baby delivering a baby.

"I wish you were home so I could tell you about it. The mother was fourteen years old. Fourteen! She screamed and yelled and scared the crap out of everyone, and then suddenly there he was."

Emily's voice quavers. Addie's own breath has become shallow, trapped in her thickening throat.

"I caught him, Mum. I caught him when he came out, and then I cut his cord with a hot knife. He was perfect, just perfect. A black swirl of hair plastered to his forehead, and scrunched up fingers. Oh, Mum. A whole, entire little life in the palm of my hand."

When was the last time Emily told her so much about anything? A whole, entire life in the palm of her daughter's hand. She has a better grasp on the baby than Addie ever could, the thought of which brings the threat of burning tears.

"I know what I want to do now, Mum. I'll try to call you again tomorrow, and we can talk about it. Might be in the middle of the night your time, though. Gotta go.... Love you, Mum."

Addie glances at the alarm clock, does a quick calculation. If she sleeps now, she might be alert enough for Emily's midnight call.

But the call doesn't come. Instead, as she lies wrapped in her grandmother's shawl, Addie cries, great, gusting sobs that surprise and frighten her. She cries for the baby who has no father, and she cries for its mother, herself a child in an orphanage. She cries for Emily, who still does not know about her father; Emily, who was the first to hold someone else's baby, but not her own. And she weeps for Darren, for their marriage that could not survive the two of them.

She opens her eyes to the heaviness of dawn, the grey sky betraying not a hint to the day's weather. Addie remembers lying in bed as a child at Buppa's house, certain she could tell by the *type* of darkness whether or not it had snowed in the night. There was always a delicious moment of anticipation before she sprang out of bed to see if she was right, if the trees and the swing set in the yard would be covered in white. Whether it was the darkness or the snow-muffled air, Addie doesn't know, but she tries, from the warmth of her bed, to resurrect that heightened sense of childish awareness.

Then she thinks of Buppa, buried in the frozen ground at the cemetery behind the church, and of Darren, or what's left of him (she cannot bring forth the word "remains") sitting in an urn. Addie wonders what Susan will do with the urn, his ashes. The small thought of whether the urn matches Susan's careful décor flits through her mind.

It is the coldness inside her that allows such thoughts, and it brings Addie to the realization that perhaps the divorce judge was wrong. Maybe Darren would have been the better parent. Maybe he could have given Emily what she needed to keep her from seeking out remote places filled with the needy and forsaken, seeking the love Addie could never fully hand over. Darren may well have been the better, more loving parent, but then he would have left Emily far too soon.

Which he has done anyway, just as Buppa did.

Much loved and deeply missed.

Guy in a Hoodie

"I AM A FAILURE as a wife and mother," Mary Beth announced, not for the first time, as we lurched across Barrington Street. I grabbed her arm to keep her from stumbling on the curb, and winced as a bolt of pain shot through my shoulder.

"You are not a failure," I said, leaning into her for balance and thinking of my sullen, beautiful Joey, home alone on his computer with a can of Pringles for company. I rubbed my shoulder and kept walking.

"In-need, in, in*deed* I am." Mary Beth stood still, swaying slightly with her index finger pointed skyward as though to prove her slurred point. "My husband left me five years ago. My daughter is a foul-mouthed teenaged shit. Ergo, I am a failure." She blinked twice behind wire-rimmed glasses, her green eyes dazed by drink.

"No, no," I replied, with a passing thought to my own slowed tongue. The fourth Black Russian I had just drained off at Smithwick's Pub had been perhaps one too many. "You are simply drunk, Mary Beth. Your husband left you be, because *he* is a shit. Your daughter is merely foul-mouthed."

For a moment we looked at each other. Mary Beth's upper lip was a darker hue than the lower, her lipstick having rubbed off earlier in the evening on a martini glass. I had the vague thought that I had just made an insensitive remark, until her dark upper lip twitched. We burst out laughing, loud guffaws of the sort we were capable of bringing about only in each other and which sent us both over to lean against the grey stone cathedral wall.

"Ouch," I erupted, as the not-yet-familiar pain seized my collarbone. Soon I would have to learn my way around it, much the same as I had learned my way around other, bigger pains in my life. The shoulder sprain was still young, only a day old from my having walked into the door to the school gym while lecturing a student about back-talk. For now I was contented to drink this particular pain down the drain.

"You oughta be more careful, Donna." Mary Beth's eyebrows furrowed. I nodded, and we kept walking, our feet plodding one before the other.

"My feet are cold," I commented, thinking that sandals hadn't been the wisest choice on an October evening. "And you know it is I who is the failure."

"*Am* the failure," Mary Beth said helpfully.

"I *are* the failure. Ha!" I guffawed at my own joke. "Thank you for confirming my sush, my suspicions. It is I whose son has dropped out of school to follow his Internet ad, adit, ad*dic*tions, and whose husband has left her for a chubby blonde. Let me be the failure tonight."

"Well, all right. But first you need to learn some grammar, for chrissake."

"Right, then, so go ahead and learn me some grammar, teacher-lady!" I was becoming breathless from walking on an incline. Bloody Halifax and its bloody hills. A Bloody Mary might help, but I was distracted from the thought by my frozen toes. "My feet are cold," I added.

"What you need is another drink," Mary Beth said. "And then your feet will *not* be cold. You know."

We kept walking, and I considered her words. I had four dollars and fifty-three cents in my pocket. Not enough for another drink.

"Besides," she continued, "we are celebrating, are we not?"

"Yes, we are, in fact, celebrating," I agreed. "Wait, what are we celebrating?"

Mary Beth fixed me with a wild stare and held an imaginary glass aloft. "We are celebrating your indush – christ. Your in*duc*tion to the club!"

"To my induction," I cried, raising my own imaginary glass.

"You, Donna, are almost, *almost* inducted to the official teacher-ladies-dumped-by-shit-husbands club!"

"And for that," I wheezed, "damn these hills. For that, we need a drink."

"No!" Mary Beth stopped suddenly, standing ramrod straight. "What we need is something special. What we need is a joint."

I stared at her, then giggled. "The last time I smoked up was, was twenty years ago, on the night Joey was conceived," I said.

"And the last time I did it was on my wedding night. Fat lot of good it did," Mary Beth spat the words.

We stopped by the library and sat on the concrete wall surrounding it. Yellow pools of light fell away from the streetlights, reflecting off the bronze back of Winston Churchill. His hands, clasped behind him, assumed greater proportions than usual in the weak light. Couples strolled past us, cars came and went, and on the lawn behind us a few clumps of teenagers hung around. Standing alone near the entrance to the library was a young guy in a black hoodie and torn jeans, tall and slight of build. His arms were crossed and his head moved to the beat of whatever was pounding through his ear buds.

"Think he's a dealer?" Mary Beth whispered, giving a nod in his direction, her breath a boozy puff.

"Could be," I said. I was not, however, going to be the one to start a conversation with some guy in a hoodie.

"Let's go talk to him, see if he's a dealer."

"And say what?" I had no desire to approach a stranger about purchasing illicit substances. I'd have said as much if I could have trusted my drunken tongue to wrap itself around all those syllables, but I couldn't, so stayed quiet.

"Ask if he's got any grass, that's what." Mary Beth looked once again in the guy's direction.

"You don't just ask, do you?"

My dearest friend in the world looked at me as though I were a dolt.

"Well, how do you think you get it, then?" she asked.

"You, well, you wait until someone hands you a joint at a party," I said. Mary Beth snorted and brought her hand to her mouth.

"I know. Me too," she squealed from behind her hand. "I've never actually bought the stuff."

We sat a few more minutes, watching people go by, until the creeping cold from the concrete wall got the better of us.

"He still there?" Mary Beth asked, rubbing her chilly behind.

"Yeah," I said, filled with sudden resolve. "I'm gonna ask him."

"You can't!" I winced and groaned as Mary Beth grabbed, and then let go my sprained shoulder. "Oh, sorry," she said, patting me on the arm. "But you just can't."

"Now who's got cold feet?" I asked. She raised her hands in denial and turned away as though looking at something interesting down the street. I left her standing by the wall as I strode over to the guy in the hoodie. The sound of her rushing footsteps followed me, and I stopped before the guy.

"Excuse me," I said in far too loud a voice, "would you happen to know where we can get some grass?"

He unfolded his arms and pulled out his earbuds, then looked around.

"You mean weed?" he asked, his eyes moving from my face to Mary Beth's and then to several points beyond us. A stubble too faint to be a goatee surrounded his thin lips like mist.

"Uh, sorry, yeah. Weed," I said, trying but failing to ignore the flush burning my cheeks. "Got any?"

"Jesus, Donna, keep your voice down," Mary Beth said, her own voice high and giggly.

"I might know a guy," he said quietly.

I reached in my purse and pulled out my four dollars and fifty-three cents.

"How much can I buy with this?" I asked in a much lower voice. The guy looked at my collection of loonies and change, frowned in disbelief, then raised an eyebrow and grinned.

"You serious? None. Half a joint, maybe."

"Damned inflation," I said, my face burning. "Listen, I have no idea what I'm doing, here. Help me out."

"How much do you want?" the guy asked, still grinning. "How 'bout an eighth?"

"How much does an eighth cost? I'll go to the bank machine." I felt more foolish by the word. He told me how much, and I grabbed Mary Beth and we rushed toward the bank at the corner. She was laughing so hard she couldn't speak.

"What the hell's an eighth," I muttered. By now I was tingling with nerves. "And what's so funny?"

"I can't believe we're doing this," she whisper-squealed, once again grabbing my arm and this time causing me to cry out in pain. I yanked the money from the ATM slot.

"What are you waiting for?" Mary Beth asked, her eyes bright with adventure. "C'mon, let's go."

"Should we be doing this?" I asked.

"Induction to the club," Mary Beth said slowly, as though speaking to a six-year-old. "Let's go."

I looked at the money in my hand and back at Mary Beth, took a deep breath, and stuffed it in my purse as we hurried back toward the library.

"What if he's gone?" Mary Beth asked.

But he wasn't.

"Okay, then. We'd like an eighth, please." I tried to ignore the pounding in my ears as I reached for the money.

"Of weed," Mary Beth added in a stage whisper.

"Let me text my buddy." He turned and walked across the lawn towards the pizza place, his thumb flying across the keypad of his cell phone. I fell into step with him, Mary Beth a few paces behind. He closed his phone with a snap.

"What's a nice lady like you want to get high for?" he asked. I told him my sorry tale, about my failed marriage, my high school dropout son, my sprained shoulder. I even told him about my cold feet.

"Jesus, you do have a lot of shit going down," he said. I nodded.

"What about you, why are you selling it?" I asked, emboldened by his sympathy.

He looked at me sideways, then back at Mary Beth. "You're not social workers, are you?" he asked.

"No, nothing like that," I laughed. But I couldn't quite bring myself to tell him we were school teachers. Maybe one of us had taught him when he was a kid.

"I didn't think so." He stepped off the curb without looking and suddenly held up his hand, keeping me from charging in front of a passing taxi. "I'm just, you know, trying to raise some cash so I can go to college. I've got a kid, see, a three-year-old, and I need a steady job. I want to do something in IT, you know?"

Before I could respond, he said, "There's my buddy. Wait here." He nodded to a burly man in a bomber jacket with a ball cap pulled low over his face, and the two of them crossed the street.

The guy in the hoodie, now known to me as a father who wanted to support his child, wasn't much older than my own son. Joey's angry eyes floated before me for a moment as I considered this.

Our guy glanced over at us. He sniffed the contents of the bag, and handed over the cash. Buddy pocketed the entire amount, and walked away into the darkness.

"C'mon, ladies, let's walk," he said as he moved swiftly past us. Mary Beth and I struggled to keep up with his long stride.

Mary Beth finally spoke. "You've been awfully kind," she said. "Come and share it with us. Only you're going to have to roll it."

The three of us found a quiet laneway behind the cathedral. In the half-light he started rolling the joint.

"Er, may I have the first puff?" Mary Beth asked, almost apologetically.

He lit the joint and handed it to her. Mary Beth hauled on it, coughed, and handed it to me. I held it to my mouth and breathed deeply. The sickly-sweet smoke invaded my throat, and I managed to stave off the urge to cough.

"It's been awhile," I whispered.

He nodded as though he'd figured as much.

"Sure has," Mary Beth said, giggling.

The three of us puffed for a few minutes.

"What kind of music you got on your iPod?" I asked.

"Rush," he told me. "Joel Plaskett. And The Beatles. Good music that makes you think about stuff."

"Hmm," I said. "I don't even know what my son listens to."

"Maybe you should ask him."

"You're right, I should," I said, handing him the joint. I should ask Joey all sorts of things, I thought, but didn't say. "When do you think you'll be able to apply for college?"

"Ah, soon, I guess. Every time I get some cash together, something comes up," he said, as he took a few quick tokes. "For now this helps pay the bills."

He walked and Mary Beth and I wobbled back out to the street. The guy popped his earbuds in place and pulled up his hood.

"Gotta go," he said. "Time to put my little guy to bed." Before I could thank him, he hiked quickly up the hill and away from us. I stared after him a moment.

"That kid is a better mother than I am," I muttered.

"No, Donna. You are the best mother to your son. Just like our *dealer* – there, I said it, just like our dealer is to his little boy." Mary Beth's mouth twitched. "Omigod, we have a *dealer!*"

"Father, not mother. You know," I said. "Him, I mean. Our guy."

"Dealer. Say it, Donna."

"Okay, our dealer. Whatever."

I looked at Mary Beth, who for the first time all evening was not on the brink of giddiness. Her eyes moved from mine to the ground and over to Winston Churchill.

"Welcome to the club," she said, her voice rough with fatigue. Her eyes were bloodshot, the green irises brilliant, which may have been from the weed, or maybe she was tearing up behind her glasses. She gave me a shrug and a small smile, one I had trouble returning.

Mary Beth looked up the hill where our guy, our *dealer*, had headed off with quick strides, hands in his pockets and hood covering his head, enjoying the cooling autumn night, plugged into his iPod.

I wondered which Beatles tune he was listening to.

Butterfly

CLIFFORD SLAMS THE DOOR, and checks that it's locked before swinging first one leg and then the other down to the pavement. With his inflamed hip he manages with some awkwardness and a grunt; it doesn't help that his beer gut gets in the way and slows him down. He blows some warmth into his cupped hands before filling the rig's tank. This morning's hard frost will do in the last of Marion's tomatoes. He hasn't had the heart to pick them, so there they sit, abandoned on the vine. Next week he will return from the Florida route to the blackened fruit and an empty home. Christ knows, snow, maybe.

A quick cup of coffee to take off the chill, and he will be on his way, with Dolly Parton for company. That woman can break a man's heart – *Here You Come Again, Heartbreak Express, I Will Always Love You.* Easy on the eyes, too; a double-D feast for a man like Clifford, who's gone without far too long. He feels a boner creeping into place and with a twinge of guilt, hitches his trousers as he saunters into the truck stop and takes the booth nearest the door.

"Cuppa coffee, hon?"

'Delores', the badge pinned to her mint-green blouse reads. Delores has a voice that could grate cheese and a mouth like a postage slot. Her hair is cut short and is the colour of faded straw. She may not be Dolly Parton, but at least she's friendly.

"Yes, please. Got a long drive ahead."

"Whereabouts you off to?"

"Florida."

"Anywheres warmer than here is okay by me," Delores rasps. "Here's a menu. Be right back." She twitches off to another table and takes the guy's order.

The door opens, letting in a cold whoosh of air. Couple of hippie kids, all braids and scarves. Jesus sandals with woolen socks, holes in the toes. What are they trying to prove, anyways, Clifford wonders. At least when he was a hippie, a *real* hippie, back in the late '60s, they were trying to do good in the world. These kids are just trying to draw attention to themselves, with their tattoos and piercings Christ-knows-where. He squints at the menu, thinks about the route to Gainesville. Always in his mind he is planning a route, driving ahead of himself to avoid surprises. Once he's driven someplace, he's got it lodged in his memory. It's a gift, like a musician's ear for a tune.

The hippies are talking quietly, looking around the room. Clifford prepares himself; any minute they'll be sidling up to try and mooch a ride. But he has a firm policy: no free rides to strangers, not after what happened to old Fred and his wife that time they picked up some nutcase hiding a stash of coke and a four-foot length of piano wire in his backpack.

"What'll it be, hon?"

Delores is back, her voice grinding like rusty gears, swishing her cloth on the formica and whisking a paper placemat and cutlery before him with the breathtaking speed of a career waitress.

"Trucker's Special, please. Over-easy on whole wheat."

"Be right up."

The hippie girl is shaking her head. Looks embarrassed. The hippie boy kisses her on the cheek, and then – Christ, what's he doing, standing on a chair and clapping his hands?

"Excuse me, hello? Everyone, could I please have your attention – hello? Excuse me?"

At which point the girl puts two fingers between her lips and shrieks a whistle that'd stop a bull. The diner is suddenly silent. Truckers in dirty ball caps turn with dubious expressions, some of them shaking their heads at the nerve of these kids.

"Uh, yeah. Um, thanks… Listen, my girlfriend and I were just wondering? You know, if any of you truck drivers who are heading south would consider taking this along with you?" The hippie holds up a shoebox for all to see. "You'd be doing us all a huge favour, you know? And…"

A voice emerges from the crowd. "You want one of us to take a box of Christ-knows-what south of the border? Are you kiddin' me, bud?"

The air rumbles with the laughter of thirty drivers as they all turn back to their breakfasts.

"Wait, no, it's nothing like that! It's a butterfly. Really."

His voice breaks on "really," but no one is listening. The drivers are far more interested in their hash browns and sausage links than what the young people have in their shoebox. The girl pulls on the hippie's sleeve, which he yanks away from her grip as he climbs down off his chair. The two of them sit miserably on stools, with the box on the counter between them. Delores raises her eyebrows and waves her coffee pot at them, but they shake their heads. Then she chats with them, and the girl lifts the shoebox lid an inch for her to peer into. Delores nods her head and pours them coffee anyway.

Clifford thinks ahead to the Florida drive. He will not drive down to East Florida, as he and Marion had planned last spring, will not be making the side trip to pay the deposit on an RV home. Their dream home. Twenty-nine-thousand saved, mostly put away from Marion's pension and disability, enough to get them and their furniture down there in time for Christmas. Marion drove with him the last time and chose the place, Magnolia Village. Nice folk, people like them who live quietly and don't expect too much of life, just a little sunshine in winter and evening card games. A few beers and a bowl of pretzels, maybe the *Tonight Show* if they're up to it.

Clifford smiles, thinking of Marion's blue eyes, her rattling, wheezing cackle every time she wins a game of euchre.

Every time she won, that is. His smile vanishes.

"Here ya go, hon. Over-easy on whole wheat. Just what the doctor ordered." Delores rips his bill off the pad and flicks it on the table, then in a lowered voice, asks him, "You said you're driving south?"

"What's that?" Clifford wonders if Delores is propositioning him, until she nods her head in the direction of the sulking hippies.

"It's a monarch they got in that box. You know, a butterfly."

"A butterfly?" Clifford blinks in disbelief.

"One of them orange and black ones you don't see so much any more. They say they rescued it, but it's getting too cold out for it to survive. Go figure, eh? Here, lemme give you a refill."

Clifford stares at the couple, then looks away, but it's too late; the girl has seen him looking, and is climbing off her stool and hurrying over to his booth, clutching the box to her thin chest. Clifford makes busy with his breakfast, and pretends not to see the hippies standing beside him.

"Sir? Sir, may I ask you something?" Her voice is oddly child-like. He wasn't expecting a 'sir' from her, and he is surprised by her overbite, which he hadn't noticed earlier.

"Hmm? What's that?" Couldn't her parents have sprung for braces, he wonders.

"Mind if we sit a minute, sir? We won't stay long, I promise, and then you can eat in peace. You know, peace?" She points at the peace symbol at her boyfriend's neck, carved wood held in place with a leather thong, above which his adam's apple bobs with nervous swallows.

"Sir, my name is Maya, and this here's my boyfriend, Robert. We have a *huge* favour to ask, if you don't mind."

Maya slides into the seat opposite him, and pulls her boyfriend with her. She has made two syllables of "huge." While she draws breath, Robert jumps in. His face looks too young for the growth of beard he's attempting on his chin.

"Yeah, it's really cool. Couple weeks ago Maya brings home this butterfly? You know, a monarch? Anyways, she found it on a fence, and it was, um, injured. He had a little tear in his wing, and Maya was so cool, she just emptied out her water bottle and put him inside with a few leaves, you know?"

"Yeah, and then I rushed home and showed it to Robert," Maya interrupts breathlessly. "I thought, surely to God there's gotta be a way to rescue this butterfly, and so I checked on the Internet."

"And she totally found it, Friends of the Monarch? A website about the migration of the monarch butterfly. Can you believe it?"

Robert looks at Clifford eagerly, then at Maya, who is gazing at him expectantly with enormous blue eyes untarnished by makeup. Clifford nods his head as though to say yes, he can believe it. Looks away from the girl's unblinking gaze. Shifts in his seat.

"There's a whole page about wing repair, so we followed the instructions and made a splint," Maya says, resting a small hand against the side of the box.

"You made a splint for a butterfly?" Clifford wonders if he's hearing right.

"Yeah, and then we fed him, you know, rotting pears and honey? Fattened him right up. It's been an amazing journey, you know?"

"And now we need you to finish the butterfly's journey," says Maya in a pleading voice.

The mention of rotting pears brings to mind Marion's frostbitten tomatoes, which this time next week will be black on the vine. Clifford brings the coffee cup to his mouth and takes a long slurp. Winces at the bitterness.

"He's been flapping around the house, and we're afraid the cat's going to eat him. There's no way he can migrate on his own without freezing, now." Robert swallows, causing his adam's apple to dance.

"Sir, we really need your help. This butterfly won't stand a chance without you. Please, sir, do you think you could take him with you?"

She clasps her pale hands and brings them to her chin.

Maya is really very pretty, with her braided hair and enormous blue eyes. The overbite lends her an appealingly vulnerable look. Christ, he thinks, looking away. She's young enough to be his granddaughter. And there's Marion, only four months in the grave. Christ, he thinks again.

Robert slides the shoebox across the table. There are holes poked in the lid in the shape of a heart.

"Wanna see Ludwig? That's what we named him. For Beethoven, right?"

"Yeah, our cat's name is Wolfgang, as in Mozart. We just love classical," Maya pipes up.

Robert eases the lid open a few inches to reveal some yellowed leaves and a twig, upon which clings the monarch, its wings opening and closing slowly to its own rhythm. The fragrance of rotting fruit makes its way from the box to Clifford, who gazes at the butterfly, wondering what in hell he's getting himself in for.

"Sure, I'll take it," he says. Across from him, Robert beams, and Maya bounces in her seat, laughing and clapping her hands.

"Aw, man, this is awesome! Thank you so much!" Robert manages. Maya leans across the table and kisses Clifford on the cheek, then turns to Robert and plants one on his mouth.

"See, I told you we'd find someone. Sir, you're the best. Just the best."

Clifford's cheek tingles where Maya kissed him. He tries not to think of it while they are exchanging cell phone numbers.

"There oughta be enough pear in there to feed him for a few days. Please, please don't let him get cold, and remember to call us the minute you release him."

Clifford and Robert shake hands, and Maya flings her arms around him. At the next booth a few sets of bristly eyebrows rise beneath baseball cap bills, but Clifford does not care.

"Thank you so much, sir. You are a kind and generous man. Take care of Ludwig for us – you're saving his life."

Ludwig, sheesh! he thinks as he zips his coat and tucks the shoebox under his arm. The girl's eyes are bright with tears as the pair leave the truck stop and climb into a rusted Gremlin, which wheezes onto the highway.

"Here, hon, take this along."

Clifford is surprised when Delores hands him a paper bag.

"You'll want a little lunch sometime," she says softly. "That's a good thing you're doing, there. Drive safe."

"Thanks," he says, holding the bag in one hand and the shoebox in the other. He must hurry to the rig before the cold air gets to the butterfly. With surprising ease he swings up into the cab and gently places the shoebox on the floor between the seats.

A bench beneath a palm tree beckons. Clifford is tired from the long haul; didn't sleep well in back of the cab last night, his hip sore from the drive. Gainesville is such a bright place, the sky a violent blue, the sidewalks glaring in the sunlight. *It's always sunny in Florida*, Marion once said, her eyes lit with the thought on a dreary March afternoon back home. Too sunny, Clifford now thinks, pulling his Deere cap low on his forehead.

He lands hard on the bench, half-growling, half-groaning. It's as good a place as any to release Ludwig. He lifts the lid and holds the box out in front of him, like an offering; gives it a shake when nothing happens; brings the box back to his lap and looks inside.

The butterfly is no longer moving, is tipped over to one side, its frayed and splinted wing pointing skyward. Clifford touches the wing and then places the box on the bench beside him. For a long time he looks at it, breathing the scent of rotted pear. Above him the palm leaves rustle and clack, tossed by a breeze. Marion had been so excited about the palm trees.

Clifford brings a callused hand to his eyes, ambushed by grief. He takes two choked breaths, and then a clean one. He wrestles the cell phone from his pocket and presses the buttons that will find the girl. *I'm here in Florida, yes… Yes, a safe drive, thanks… Good weather here…* Clifford tells her what she wants to hear, the words he needs to say. Her squeals and laughter help make up for his lie. He can just see her pretty blue eyes, her braided hair.

Clifford lays the phone on top of the shoebox, stretches his legs, and unzips his jacket. He can't complain about being warm in November. Already his hip feels better; must be the warm air.

Maybe he'll just stay here awhile.

Scars

IN THE SHED BEHIND the barn there hangs a strap. It bears the scuffs and scratches of countless thrashings, mine and my brothers' repentant and not-so-repentant arses ingrained in the leather. At one end of it there is an oily stain, an impression of my father's hand, his fingers, his grasp. At the other end protrude two sharp, blackened furniture tacks, each bent back to form an iron 'U'.

I don't often come here anymore, and I wouldn't have bothered if not for my brother Johnny's insisting. If it had been either of the other two, I might have stayed back and let them sell the place without me, but I trust Johnny to know what to do. He always did know, right from the start.

Through the doorway I glimpse the shingled house, all traces of white paint stripped off by weather and time. Two of its three windows are broken, dirty sheers blocking the sun's entry to the kitchen. This is the place where meals were cooked and devoured, lessons taught and learned. We boys took our first steps here, and at the kitchen table we read our first words from Mother's cracked and thumb-worn bible. We learned our prayers; and at meals and before bed, also before thrashings, we spoke them, words of forgiveness and redemption: *Heavenly Father, forgive me for my sins....* We were taught how to use a gun.

My brothers and I learned to drive in the back lot, and in the barn we played hockey and learned about sex, rifling through ill-gotten *Playboy* magazines. We drank our first beer, smoked our first joint, and most of us groped our first adolescent-female breasts in the loft, enveloped in the sickly-sweet scent of hay and risk, always the risk of being caught.

This is the place of my birth, and of my father's death. It was once my home.

✧

We all bear the scars of risk.

Zinnia, my mother, walked with a crutch, her left leg ruined from being thrown by a horse. The leg was amputated at the knee, and an ill-fitting peg strapped to what remained.

My eldest brother, Matthew, has only one eye, the other destroyed by a wayward pellet. Johnny, the youngest of us, will only speak if he's had enough to drink, which is sometimes to say far too much, and Luke, his twin, cannot control his mouth.

My wife sometimes traces the strap's pathways across my back. As I grow older, she tells me, the shiny white trails are fading.

Luke and Johnny hated each other from an early age. With their dense black curls and startling blue eyes, they were a constant reminder to our mother of her only brother, Jean-Luc. Mother idolized Jean-Luc, who carried his lame sister on his shoulders and taught her how to ride again. He defended her honour against bullies and cads, and showed her how to plant her knee and to throw a snowball with deadly accuracy so that she might defend herself from the bullies during the winter he went to war.

Zinnia never recovered from her brother's death overseas. She married one of the local bullies, a remote man named Wayne Frommer, and promptly gave him two boys. Matthew was first, blue-eyed and an easy child. I was next, a difficult birth and a colicky baby, as Mother often reminded me.

Sarah, our sister, died at six months of crib death. For four years Zinnia begged her husband for one more, desperate for the company of a girl. One drunken evening, Wayne gave in, and eight months later the twin boys were born. Mother buried her disappointment deep, considering it God's wish that she find herself surrounded by five males, so she named the twins for her beloved brother.

Johnny and Luke didn't stand a chance with her.

My father had a strict house rule, and that was that no one under the age of ten was allowed anywhere near his rifle collection, which he kept under lock-and-key in a cabinet over the Frigidaire, well out of reach of curious little hands. Every year he'd go off with his cousins into the bush for a week, and bag his deer quota to feed us for a while. Later on, he'd tell us of his hunting escapades. Matt and I were transfixed by his descriptions of the right moment, the second of absolute certainty when he had the deer lined up in his sights, and how the deer would glance his way as if it knew this was its last moment on earth.

Father never missed, and he never had an accident. Throughout our childhood, he would tantalize us by saying, "When you're old enough, I'll show you how it's done."

Matthew began his training at the age of ten. Every night after supper, Father would fish around on his key ring until he found the key to the rifle cabinet. With certain ceremony he'd open the glass door, and with both hands, lower the pellet gun. I watched, silent and burning with envy as Father worked with Matt, cleaning, loading, unloading, and cleaning, over and over again. I had all the steps memorized long before Matt could perform them properly. Secretly I ached for Father's undivided attention, his unspoken approval as, over time, Matt's small hands grew more proficient in their task. Finally, when Matt could clean, load, and unload blindfolded, Father took him out to the pasture behind the orchard, where he'd set up tin cans along the fence as targets. I wasn't allowed to come along and watch, and when I raised my voice in protest, Father shouted that I'd better keep quiet and do as he said, if I ever wanted to learn how to shoot.

The mystery of Matt's shooting sessions sent me into agonies of jealousy. At night while Matt snored in his bed opposite mine, I lay with my jaw clenched, imagining Father's large hand tousling Matt's hair with every successful firing of the gun.

"Well done, Son," he might say through the pipe stem held firmly between his teeth. Matt would beam up at him, pride swelling his small chest and sending sparks of adoration from his enormous blue eyes. The reality was, after most shooting sessions they would return, first Matt rushing through the kitchen white-lipped, his reddened eyes avoiding the rest of us. Father would catch the door before it slammed shut, and slowly shake his head at the sound of Matt's feet pounding up the stairs.

"He's coming along, Zinn, but slowly," he'd say to Mother, then he'd return the pellet gun to its place in the cabinet, help himself to a beer from the Frigidaire, and sit, brooding, on the easy chair.

This went on for a few weeks until finally, one day after a rifle practice, Matt wrenched the door open and stood there, his face white and his eyes red, a candle of snot dripping from his nose. Father followed close behind, holding the rifle pointed to the floor.

"Christ! Are you crying?" Father waited for an answer that wouldn't come. "You don't want to shoot? Well then, tell me what to do with you, Matthew. Just tell me!"

Matt sniffed back the snot and walked stiffly across the kitchen and up the stairs.

Father turned to my mother, who was sitting at the table with her hand on her crutch. I don't know what he said next, because I then slipped up the stairs after Matt.

It seemed the days preceding my tenth birthday slowed to a crawl, and in fact had gone into reverse, but the day finally came when Father would show me how to clean the pellet gun. I hurried through the presents and the cake, barely noticing the triple layers Mother had glued together with my favourite chocolate frosting, and I absentmindedly spat out the wax-papered quarter.

"Aww, Dave always gets the quarter," Luke whined.

"Hush, you, it's his birthday, not yours." The lines between Mother's eyes deepened. Luke folded his arms and slumped in his chair.

"Well, boy, it's time you learned how to clean a gun," Father finally said, wiping his moustache and reaching for his pipe. Too eagerly, I jumped up from the table, knocking over my chair.

"Lord save us, David, would you for once slow down!"

"Sorry, Mother," I said, righting the chair.

Father clinked his key ring until he found the right key. I was suddenly struck with the urge to pee, but passed it off as excitement as Father took an inordinate amount of time to unlock the cabinet and lower the gun to the kitchen table. He showed me the steps to cleaning the gun, steps I had memorized from Matt's training and which whirled through my brain at ten times the speed Father was speaking. Finally it was my turn. Father placed the gun before me, its barrel glistening, waiting for me to dismantle and clean it. With sweating hands I reached for it, and as soon as I touched the cool metal, the need to pee became desperate.

"Just a minute," I muttered, dashing from the kitchen.

"David? David!"

"I'll be right back," I yelled down the stairs. Once before the toilet, stage fright set in and nothing happened. I thought of the gun sitting, waiting on the table, and of Father's certain growing impatience. I hopped up and down, and turned on the tap for inspiration. Finally, my bladder co-operated. I washed but did not dry my hands, and flew back down the stairs.

When I returned to the kitchen, Father was turning the key in the cabinet. The table was bare.

"Wait, I..."

"I need your undivided attention." Father's voice was cold.

"But I had to..."

"I don't care if you had to put out a fire in the living room, David. Guns get your full attention."

With that, he clamped his teeth around the pipe stem, and slammed out the door.

Father's cancer helped itself to his liver long before the doctors found it, and only when he suddenly became diabetic did they realize it was also feasting on his pancreas. Mother bore the responsibility of his illness with a devotion that astounded us boys. Throughout our version of their marriage, we had only known a stiff, formal tolerance between them. At best, they agreed on things, but at worst, a terrible silence would descend, paralyzing the entire family and causing us to tiptoe around each other so as not to cause any friction that might ignite our parents' tempers. Always the strap weighed on our minds; we brothers watched and waited until the silent storm was over, before resuming our usual push-and-shove banter.

She tended to him night and day, cooking more varied and simpler meals as his appetite waned, changing the sheets sometimes twice a day to ensure their freshness while he slept, and often sitting through the night, staring at a book, or at her mending. Once I saw her holding Father's hand, smiling down at him while he spoke.

Father's final task was to show the twins how to clean and load the pellet gun, their tenth birthday arriving on a slightly better day than he'd had in a while. There he sat, gaunt and yellow, trying to show the boys how to do it. Matt and I watched, appalled, as his thin and shaking fingers failed.

"I know! I know!" Luke cried out, grabbing at the barrel.

"Stop it, Luke." Matt seized Luke's wrist in his strong hand. Johnny sat back in his chair, hunched and miserable with an understanding of Father's illness that neither Luke nor I possessed.

"But I know how to do it!"

"Never mind. Let Father show you." Matt's voice was a low growl.

Father looked at Matt from beneath his bruised-looking eyelids.

"Matthew, you're the eldest. You show them," he said, his voice hoarse with fatigue. Matt's face was stricken.

"No, Dad. You know best, you do it."

"Matthew..."

Matt turned away from the table, giving me a plain view of his face from my position at the door. He bit his lip. Shook his head.

There was a long silence, one I couldn't do anything about as I stood there, frozen. My stomach lurched as I recognized rare tears springing up in Matt's eyes, as they had done all those years ago when he didn't want to learn to shoot. His face crumpled, but he kept his back straight and breathed evenly, so as not to let on to Father and the twins.

"David, then. Show the boys."

"Me? Uh, sure, Dad."

Somehow my voice co-operated along with the rest of me, as I moved to the table. I stared at the pellet gun, which for a long moment became a foreign object, something I'd never seen before in my life.

"C'mon, Dave, show us. Father said!" Luke's high-pitched whine brought me back into the kitchen.

"David, you know your way," said Father. I nodded my head, which sang with his approval, and sat between the boys. The words and the motions came easily. *I knew my way.*

Johnny was quickest, loading and unloading with dexterity and efficiency that belied his ten years, while Luke struggled and grew impatient, his voice finally rising in a wail.

"Johnny always does things first. It's no fair!" he sobbed as, for the fifth time in a row, he bungled his task. Johnny looked at the floor, then slid out of his chair and dashed up the stairs. I might otherwise have cuffed Luke, but the strain on Father's face kept me still and, at least outwardly, patient in my seat.

"Don't worry about it, Luke," Matt said from across the kitchen, his voice now restored to its seventeen-year-old baritone. "It took me a long time to get the hang of it, too, man. A lot longer than Dave, and he's two years younger than me. I'll show you a few tricks next time."

"It'll come soon enough, Lukey-boy. When you're ready."

Luke stared, open-mouthed, as Father reached over and touched his black curls, placing his large hand on the shiny jumble, and tousling. My eyes filled with unbidden, though not entirely unhappy tears.

He died one afternoon while we boys were at school. Luke arrived home first, followed by me and Johnny. The ambulance had come and gone, taking Father's corpse but leaving behind the stench of his dying.

From her seat at the table Mother stared as we walked into the kitchen, the skin drawn tight like a wax membrane across her face. She grasped the crutch with both hands, her knuckles like bleached walnuts while Lukey stood nearby, silent and pale with his hands twisting over each other, moving from one foot to the other. A long silence filled the room until finally Mother spoke.

"He died, your father. He's gone, now."

My breath caught in my throat and the top of my head tingled in a complicated wave of shock and relief that left me speechless. Lukey sniffled and added a jiggling foot to his agitated dance, while Johnny walked calmly to our mother and put his arms around her. She sat rigid and looked for a moment as though she would shoo him off and scold him. Then her shoulders slumped and she leaned forward and put her face in her hands.

This was the scene that greeted Matt when he walked through the door. He must have known right away that Father had died, for he sank onto one of the kitchen chairs and without bothering to hide it, wept long, heaving sobs.

The sour scent of death hung off the walls for weeks, despite Mother's leaving the windows open through the cold November. When the first snow came swirling through the kitchen, Johnny went quietly through the house and closed all the windows. Mother sat watching him, her hand on her crutch and her eyes flooded with sorrow.

I've never forgiven myself for taking over the twins' training. Johnny never wanted to hunt, and Luke was too impetuous. I should have known better.

"Your father would want them to know how, David," Mother said, and her word was good enough for me, so I took them out to the pasture behind the orchard, and lined up the tin cans along the fence. One after another, Johnny popped them off, more in an effort to be done with it than to show off. Luke, of course, didn't see it that way, and when his turn came he missed every single can. I expected his usual screaming and whining, but he surprised me by laying the gun down and walking away.

"Luke? Hey, Lukey, c'mon back," I called after him. "Let's do it one more time. This time you'll get it for sure."

But Luke kept on walking. With his shoulders sagging and his head down, he looked more than ever like Johnny, who was by now sitting on a tree stump, hunched and miserable.

"Good job, buddy," I said to him. "You've got a great shot."

"I don't want to shoot anymore," Johnny replied, looking at the ground.

"S'okay, Johnny, you don't have to. Come on, let's go see if lunch is ready."

I picked up the gun, and we made our way through the orchard.

Matt was talking to Luke while Mother dished up bowls of soup. She pursed her lips at Johnny as he took his place at the table.

"Luke says you were showing off, John."

Johnny opened his mouth to speak, but then closed it.

"Not exactly, Mother," I said carefully. I fished around in my pocket for the key to the gun cabinet. The key slipped from my grasp; I laid the gun down on the table to go at the key ring with both hands.

"Vanity is a sin," she said sharply. "I'll have none of it."

"You did so show off," Luke muttered. Johnny scowled.

"Did not."

"Yes, you did! You fired off every one of those cans just to bug me, just like this."

Before I could react, Luke leapt from his chair and grabbed the pellet gun. Which, for the only time in my life, I had neglected to unload.

"Lukey..." I shouted, but he had already cocked it, and was pointing it out the window as Johnny grabbed his wrist. The barrel swung away from the window in slow motion, in an impossibly long moment during which I wondered why in hell I couldn't seem to do anything useful or heroic, such as move. The time lapse between the explosion and Mother's scream seemed almost ridiculous.

Then it all speeded up as Matt slumped to the floor, clutching his eye and groaning.

The twins' screams ring in my mind as I stare at the strap. When Mother was finished beating them bloody, it was my turn, for refusing to beat them for her. In silence I removed my shirt and lowered my jeans, and knelt facing away from her. The words came easily.

"Heavenly Fath – *uhh* – Father, forgive me for my – *ahh* – for my sins..."

I accepted her harsh words, her accusations, and her thrashing, and afterward as I lay on my stomach, waiting for the sting to kick in, I thought of Matt lying in the hospital with half his face bandaged and his remaining blue eye swollen and bewildered.

My mother's voice crept into my awareness:

"Heavenly Father, forgive me for my sins..."

I peered around behind me to see her kneeling painfully, with her peg-leg resting against the wall and the strap before her on the floor, and then I was bewildered.

The strap hangs before me now, stiff and cracked. I pull it off the wall, and place my palm over the darkened imprint of my father's hand. But for my thumb, which is longer than his was, it's a perfect fit.

Boys in a Wagon

With excerpts from Geoffrey Payzant's "Courage" (2000)

A SOLDIER STANDS AT attention, weeping amid the ruins of bombed-out Bristol, tall in his sailor suit.

He was brave, once, showed courage during the crossing, hardships amidships. Such cold he had never known; the hunger; the adrenaline surge when Action Stations were called, claxons cawing while he raced to his station from the engine room (forbidden territory, but a magnet to him – the steam, the oily reek of moving parts, the throbbing roar of the engines), tumbling up ladders and through closing portals, smashing his watch en route, arriving at his station breathless, utterly without breath. No one noticed.

Now the soldier stands tall in the rubble, a working-class neighbourhood bombed flat. Houses destroyed, suppers interrupted, lullabies cut off mid-verse – the crime being the location, too close to the docks.

Two small boys have long departed, but the sound of their wagon stays with him, will always stay with him, lifelong counterpoint to the roar of ships' engines.

There approached a rattling and squeaking old wagon with one boy pulling it, by means of a rope, and another boy sitting in it.

Boys in a wagon, outside playing. But not.

They were aged perhaps six or seven years, but in a war zone it is never easy to guess the ages of children.

Maybe they were older. Who knows? The soldier stands aside to let the boys pass.

As they drew nearer I could see that the pulling boy had no eyes and the sitting boy had no legs.

Shore leave, for most soldiers, consists of days and nights spent in noisy pubs, in brothels, drinking themselves senseless, that they might erase such sights. The weeping soldier has no such mechanism. His own shore leaves are spent exploring the shadows of churches, cathedrals, seeking organs of a different type from his comrades, pouring his soul into the keys, the pedals, opening the stops so that Bach and Buxtehude's fugues may soar from him, cleanse him. The rattle-and-squeak of the wagon changes all that.

He pulls from his gas mask case his last two "nutties," and the boys thank him solemnly and put the chocolate bars in a safe corner of the wagon. Will they eat the rare sweets? Sell them? Trade? The boys give him no clear answer.

Their main preoccupation was keeping clear of "The Welfare," people who would take charge of them and separate them so that one could be taken care of in an institution for blinded children, the other in one for crippled children. Of the bombing, of their rescue, of their hospitals and foster homes, the boys would say nothing.

Bit by bit the soldier learns from them of shelters where they might find a meal, a bath, some castoff clothing.

One such shelter was a church basement (all that survived of the church) which the sitting boy pointed out; the rector, they said, was a very kind man who would never betray them to The Welfare.

They spend their days trolling the ruins, fishing for shiny scraps they might sell to a man with a barrow. The sitting boy calls out when something catches his eye, and the pulling boy then feels around for it and adds it to their pile of treasure in the wagon.

The sitting boy did not take up a lot of space.

The boys take their leave and return to work, rattle-and-squeak. The soldier would give them everything he owned, if he could. Instead he stands at attention and salutes them, weeping. His shoulders rise in rhythm to his quiet sobs; soon the front of his sailor suit is soaked with tears. He has never seen such courage.

Boys in a wagon, outside playing. But not.

Duncan's Lament

WHEN BEATRICE FIRST FOUND him it was a day like most, given the season. Above, gunmetal clouds were buffeted by the wind, accompanied by the squalling of seabirds.

Where land cut away to the sea, Beatrice paused and with eyes the colour of ice, she regarded the gulls as they soared and dipped and hovered. The powerful arc of their flashing wings held the wind, their soulless cries uttering from wide yellow beaks, while below, the waves receded from the shore, allowing her passage. Low tide following a storm leaves treasures among the stones: kindling, fishing buoys, bits of rope. Perhaps an oar, or a glass bottle. Kelp for drying.

A copper curl, loosed by the breeze, darted about her face. Beatrice tucked it back and with her eyes closed she counted the waves, timing them with the rhythm of her breath. A child's game, nothing more than a moment of rest until a brother's shout startled her back to her task. As though stung, Beatrice removed her hands from where they rested on her twitching belly, and with pounding heart she hurried, mindful of the changing tide below, of her brothers' contempt for her. The basket slapped against her back as she clambered heavily, leather straps slack across her shoulders. The wind caught her shawl, which she grasped with one chapped hand and tugged back into place, the other hand ready to catch at stone should she slip on her way down to the shore. Once on the beach she began to fill the basket, tossing in driftwood sticks and ropey lengths of kelp, watching the ground always. Not once did she stumble among the rocks, nor did she miss her target, and as the basket filled, the leather straps pulled at her shoulders. From between the stones came the fragrance of low tide, of salt and sand and the cold northern waters. The tang of fish long dead.

Suddenly, before her lay a coffin, misshapen and impossibly small. Beatrice stumbled and cried out in fright, the weight of her basket pushing on her. She stared at the coffin, and then with salt-stung hands she reached toward it. A low moan stopped her, and looking beyond, Beatrice saw a man lying in the sand. He stared at her with eyes dark as well-water, half-crazed and pleading. Again she cried out.

"Doan' touch ma fiddle," came his harsh croak. He tried to stand, bearded, mad-eyed and with wild black hair, and was immediately wracked with coughing that forced him back onto the ground.

Beatrice turned to flee, slipping her arms free of the leather straps. The basket fell, its contents spilling on the sand. She moved with quick, frantic steps, and then stopped as the man's coughing continued, jerking his prostrate form among the stones. Beatrice sized him up. A sorrier specimen she hadn't seen since her brother William had dragged Big Reg home, raging drunk and barely alive after the pummelling he'd taken from the miner whose ancestors he had insulted. Before her now lay a wild man, bloodied and half-dead from his battle with the sea. The tide was coming in. Without her help he would surely die.

"Come on, then," she said, grasping his scrawny arm and hoisting him to his feet, ignoring the foul smell of him. Even standing stooped, leaning against her, he was taller than her brothers, and when she reached around his waist all there was to hold onto was the knob of his hip. Beatrice shoved the fiddle case into the basket, slung it over her shoulders, and half-dragged the man along the shore away from the returning tide.

In answer to her cries, first William and then Angus scrambled down to her, followed by Robbie and lastly, Big Reg. William, the eldest, stared at the wreck of a man and then at Beatrice, whose pale eyes met his in a silent plea. At William's nod, her flame-haired brothers, large and forceful, had the wild man up the cliff and into the house, where they undressed and washed him. Beatrice dried his hair and then dried it again, wringing the life back into him, and fed him whiskey before the fire. All the while he clasped the fiddle case to himself and stared out over the water, his head cocked as though listening.

Beatrice allowed herself a moment of stillness, but all she could hear was the wind and the pulsing of waves below the cliff. "Ya come from the sea, ya kin work on the sea," she said to him. "You'll fish. I'll mind the children." The sorrow in his eyes failed to move her.

In the peeling white church that might not last another winter before tumbling into the sea, they were wed. Beatrice's dowry, a cow, seven chipped plates, and a woollen blanket, would do to get them started.

Not half a year passed when, in the cabin built by her scowling brothers in haste and well away from the cliff,

Beatrice screamed once, and then again. On a rug near the hearth, with the wind pouring through gaps between the logs, she birthed her first son. While she washed up the blood and wound rags between her legs, Duncan stared at the scrawny child. Slowly he opened his fiddle case and removed the splintered remains of another life. All that was left intact was the ebony fingerboard; this he snapped off from the violin's warped neck and placed on a high shelf. The rest of the fiddle he tossed into the fire without a backward glance.

Duncan took the child from Beatrice and laid him in the fiddle case, and placed it before the hearth for warmth. Then he spoke the baby's name: Neil.

Beatrice watched the adoration bloom from her black-haired husband. Then she looked at the child. His tuft of orange curls and angry red fists betrayed him, but only to Beatrice, who buried the truth of his father deep and prayed no one would notice.

Four more times Beatrice produced boys, all of them born robust and with their father's wild, dark eyes and hair. Duncan placed each baby inside the fiddle case before the fire and then spoke his name: William. Angus. Robbie. Reginald. Each was named for one of Beatrice's brothers, the men who had helped save his life and built a home for his family. And with each naming she shuddered, wincing as though struck.

Her days began long before sunrise with the fire to coax, ice to smash in the basin, and the day's bread to knead, rise, and pound again before baking. From the rocky earth came potatoes, carrots and cabbage, miracles of Beatrice's tending, battling the starved soil with dried kelp and manure from the cow. Day after day she hoed and dug and hauled rocks away from her precious crops.

From the skinny cow she managed to squeeze just enough milk. Sometimes it took an hour to fill the pail, and occasionally Beatrice emerged bruised from the shed. One time the cow kicked the pail over. Beatrice seized the nearest thing, her hoe, and flogged the bawling, stamping creature which then refused to give milk for days, despite Beatrice's desperate pulling. Never again did she strike the cow, although when the pail was tipped over from time to time, her screams mingled with the gulls' cries over the water.

It was Baby Neil, the first-born, upon whom Duncan lavished attention where Beatrice could not. Neil, who remained small, soon smaller than the rest, and whose vacant stare and clenched fists tore at Duncan's shame-ridden heart. Child of his dreams, of the past he yearned for, the present that never came; doomed from the beginning, Neil never spoke, but mewled instead like an ailing cat. Duncan carried the boy on his back in one of Beatrice's baskets, lined with wool and rebuilt so the child's skinny legs dangled from small holes, his large head propped against the side, orange curls poking out over the top. Most days Duncan carried little Neil in his basket down to the water's edge, carefully placing him in the bow of the dory before pushing off for the day's fishing. Beatrice, in her frenzy to manage her chores and the other four demanding, raucous boys, had no use for the limp, useless one.

Once, when Neil was in his first days and drowning in her milk, Beatrice had thrust the child at Duncan, screaming it was best to let him die.

"For the love of God, take him outside," she had cried. "Leave him in the snow."

Duncan wrapped the baby and left the house, holding him close against the sleet. With pounding heart he regarded the snow drifted against the cow shed. Slowly he walked toward it, his knees having turned to water and his breath coming in scraping gasps. But then there was a sound from the shed, the moaning of the cow and the shuffling of her hooves. Duncan hurried past the snow drift and kicked the door open. He carried little Neil inside, and with great tenderness he soaked a piece of woollen rag in the cow's milk and coaxed the mewling infant to suck.

And so, knowing his wife could spare no time for her crippled child, Duncan propped him up in the bow of the dory and sang to him the songs of his father and his grandfather while he fished.

Always Baby Neil's ice-blue eyes brightened at the rise and fall of his father's voice and the meaning of his words. But when land came near and the songs drew back like the tide, their brightness faded.

It was late afternoon. The sun hung low on the horizon, and from the ground came the awakening scent of the day's thaw, when Beatrice banged her cast-iron pot with a wooden spoon. From all directions came her strapping boys, William and Angus bearing wood to stack by the door, and

Robbie dragging a squalling Reg by his sleeve from the shed, where the cat had hidden six new kittens. Duncan and the baby, as she still thought of Neil, and more importantly, the day's catch, were nowhere in sight. She had used the last of the cod in a watery stew, heads, eyes, and fins floating among potato pieces. Without fish, it would be cabbage soup and bread, and not for the first time. With a strength borne of fury, Beatrice struck the spoon against the pot. The spoon splintered, and she stared at what remained of it in her hand. For Beatrice, anger was never far from worry. Like all fishermen's wives, she carried the knowledge that at day's end her husband might not return to her.

Their faces grim with apprehension, the boys lined up at the basin and scrubbed their hands in tepid water rimed with a film of grease. They waited in silence while Beatrice ladled steaming fish stew into bowls.

"You'll say grace, William, as your father's not here to do it."

William opened his mouth to speak.

"Go on, then. What are you waiting for?"

Beatrice's fury hummed beneath her words. Under the planks Angus kicked his older brother.

"F-for what we are about to receive may the Lord make us truly thankful, amen."

"Amen," muttered the others, wary of their mother's mood.

Wordlessly they ate, slurping the stew and tearing off bits of crusty bread to sop the juices. Beneath the table's planks Angus' swinging foot again caught William's shin. William passed along the nudge to Robbie, who covered his grin with a chapped hand and then tapped Little Reg's foot.

Around and around, out of their mother's sight and in silence, the brothers' feet carried their message: *All is well.* Only once did Reg, the youngest, drop his spoon.

"Sorry, Mam," said Robbie, coming to his brother's aid and diving for the spoon.

The door swung open, and again the spoon clattered to the floor. Duncan's lanky form filled the doorway with Neil dozing in his basket, his head flopped to one side, a thin glisten of drool threading from his opened mouth. On the ground, tied with rope, was the better part of a tree trunk.

"The catch, where is the catch?" Beatrice's voice pierced the silence. The answer hung in the air, unspoken, as Duncan looked past her to his four sons.

"Give us a hand, boys," he said quietly.

The two eldest rushed to help drag the trunk inside.

"Are we to eat the tree, then?" Beatrice shouted.

The boys stopped short, looking from their mother's ashen face, her eyes bright with rage, to their father, and back. Duncan spoke in a low voice.

"Before the fire, to help it dry."

The boys moved carefully toward the log. Beatrice breathed deeply once. Then, in her terrible silence, she placed a bowl of stew at the head of the table.

For weeks the spruce log dried. Each morning it was shoved out of the way of her cooking by Beatrice, and later on moved back by Duncan. Every night Duncan ran his hand over the rough-hewn end, stroked his beard, and then he turned it over so the other end might dry further.

At last it was time for Duncan to take up his knife and chisel. Night after night while Beatrice mended the nets, he carved by lamplight, with Baby Neil gazing from his basket nearby. Under Neil's watchful eyes the fiddle took shape, a thistle growing at one end of it. The thistle annoyed Beatrice, who wondered aloud more than once why Duncan couldn't make it look like a regular fiddle, with a simple scroll at the top like the one her father had played. Duncan had merely smiled sadly and looked at the floor.

The hours he spent carving and polishing took Duncan further from Beatrice, cast him back to his earlier, unknowable life before his appearance on the rocky shore, before she had rescued them both from their pasts.

"Who was he, Duncan, who was Neil named for?" Beatrice once asked, her words scored by irritation.

"I once had a brother, Neil, and now I haven't. Better ya doan' know more," was his careful reply before he delved deeper into the secrets of the spruce.

At last it was ready to sing. In the dawn's frosted shadows, Duncan slipped outside with the fiddle case tucked under his arm. He settled on the milking stool in the shed, and while the cow shuffled about in the nearby pen, he lowered his head as though in prayer. Finally, he eased the case open and smoothed his callused hand over the varnish, pausing at the thistle crowning the fiddle's neck. So long ago, and so far away, his grandfather's thistle had stayed with him, had made the voyage across an ocean and away from one family, moving on with him to another.

In a swift motion, Duncan tucked the fiddle beneath his chin. With his other hand he grabbed the bow, placing horsehair on string. Beads of sweat steamed on his forehead, and the only sound was of his breath whistling in and out of his nose. Finally he moved his hand and drew the bow across the string.

At first it pranced and skittered out of control like an unbroken horse, Duncan's fingers protesting, stiff and cold and filthy from his years of fishing. For too long he had been away from his old fiddle, and his ear, refined from a lifetime of tunes heard first at his grandfather's knee, objected to the squawks and groans of the new one. He stopped and tried to breathe some warm air onto his hands.

From the pen came a moaning crescendo as the restless cow gazed at him. Duncan laid the fiddle in its case, dragged the stool over to the cow, and hauled at her teats with awkward fingers until her milk flowed and his hands began to warm. When the pail was filled, he glanced at his hands. Fish grime was permanently lodged beneath his fingernails and etched in the creases and folds of his knuckles, and had been, according to Beatrice, one more thing to keep him from Godliness. Duncan reached for the steaming pail and touched one blackened fingertip to the white froth. Not a moment passed before he plunged both hands into the milk. All thoughts of Godliness left him as he threw back his head and gasped. The creamy warmth filled him, and later, while the sun came up, his fiddle sang.

"Mam? Mam," came the soft cry. With a start, Beatrice opened her eyes and sat up. The shadow of a son, her youngest, stood at the door, whimpering as the fiddle's first cry emerged from the darkness.

"What is it, child?" Beatrice registered a familiar tune wending through the pounding of her heart, causing her feet to twitch, echoing steps not danced in so many years. Little Reg whimpered and threw himself at her. Beatrice frowned, and after a moment put her arms around his thin shoulders.

"Do ya hear it, Mam?"

"Yes, Reggie. Yes, I hear it."

"Neil says…" A sob choked Little Reg's words.

"Neil says what?" Beatrice said sharply. Neil had never, ever spoken, not once in his life.

"Neil says it's Papa."

"Foolishness." Beatrice considered the impossibility of Neil speaking his first word, Neil with his slack jaw and his hopeless baby sounds.

Then she considered the possibility of it, and wept.

She eased the shed door open so as not to make a sound. The back of her husband faced her, his skinny shoulders stooped as he embraced the fiddle, and his hair, every which way as always, bobbing with the effort of the reel he was playing. Again Beatrice felt the steps moving in her feet. When Duncan finished the tune he breathed deeply once, and coughed. Beatrice took a step forward, and then stopped as he began the slow, keening melody of a lament.

For a long time Beatrice stood there listening with her eyes closed, imagining the anguish of Duncan's lament being carried on the backs of seabirds and out over the waves. In her husband's music she heard the pain of his losses, of the family he'd left behind before washing up on her shore; and she heard the pain of his love, the tenderness he carried for Neil, the son who wasn't his and yet was more his own than anyone else's, even Beatrice herself.

When the last note faded away, Beatrice opened her mouth to speak, but no words would come. As she moved toward him, Duncan turned with a start, his dark eyes red-rimmed and ashamed. The sight of him blurred in the fog of her tears.

"I'll not play it again, Beatrice," he said, as he reached for the fiddle case.

She laid her hand on his wrist, felt his pulse fluttering beneath her fingers, and lifted his arm until the bow touched the strings.

"Please, Duncan," she said. "Please."

Storey's Keeper

IN THE COLD DARKNESS of night, Walter stares at the empty pillow, studying what he once knew of his lover's profile, the slight rise in the bridge of his nose, his parted lips, a deviated septum keeping them from sleeping in silence. Walter minded then, but now, even in the quiet, he is awake, so he may as well pretend to do what he once did: gaze upon his beloved Jeremy.

With the days shortening into autumn, morning light comes later and later. As always, Walter greets the day by staring at the empty pillow beside him.

The view from Walter Storey's window is clear. Tilly has done a good job of cleaning the glass, leaving not a streak, not a fingerprint, just as he likes it. Air gone clear and hard.

"Clean as a whistle, Perfessor," she'd remarked, triumph broadening her grin as she gave the window a final polish.

Below him the street is busy with the usual bustle of traffic, both pedestrian and automotive. A young man with a thick braid snaking down his back lopes along, Starbucks in hand and an oversized backpack draped over one shoulder. Probably a university student, although not one of his. Walter would remember the braid. The student passes an executive-looking woman walking the other way, her stride confined by her tight skirt and heels. She is half a block from the intersection. Walter wonders if she'll take the extra five minutes to walk through the park and admire the hydrangea, which must be in full, towering bloom by now. The Number Seven bus rumbles by. Everything is as it should be.

Walter clenches his rear end, adjusts his trousers and smoothes the crease. He leans back against the chair's scratchy softness, settles into a familiar ache radiating from the sternum outward, ribs, collarbone, sciatic nerve accounted for. Physical comfort, forsaken during a moment of screeching tires and pounding air bags, is a thing of the past, a fond memory tucked away with other, greater losses; with Jeremy. The curve of his back has worn into the upholstery – perhaps it's time to re-cover the armchair. The chocolate tweed depresses him. Maybe something lighter, moss green, or even a buttery yellow. Tilly might have an opinion. Walter smiles at the thought.

Tilly, dear Tilly. He'll forgive her the vile soups and rubber-egg lunches as long as she keeps his window clean; as long as she fills the apartment with her opinions and happy chatter. Tilly, with her face as straightforward as her proclamations, framed with the beginnings of jowls at one end and a graying fringe draping the other. With her big-soled running shoes and faded golf shirts she seems out of place in his austere apartment, ready to topple the delicate art deco nude standing on a plinth by the piano – hell, she's ready to topple the piano, really. But twice a day, six days a week, she is his family. Mornings she brings in groceries, cleans, helps him with his exercises. Cooks him his lunch. Afternoons she spends elsewhere. Walter sometimes wonders, with a twinge of possessiveness, exactly who wins Tilly's attention during the hours she is out. But as long as she is back at 6:00 to get supper and make sure he takes his pills before bed, he's satisfied. Always at breakfast she folds back the newspaper, usually the Life section, and circles some story for him to read, as if he hasn't already read it in the dark hours of the dawn.

This morning's story was circled not once, but twice. "Balls!!" read the margin note scribbled in red pen alongside the headline, the ink as much carved into the paper as written.

"Memory Reaches No Further than the Fifth Year of Life," blared the headline. The article was full of statements about the limited cognitive abilities in toddlers, children's later ability to fabricate the past. Walter had chuckled as he dug through the scrambled egg using his fork as a saw. He knew Tilly'd like that one.

Sure enough, after lunch she'd given him an earful.

"I don't know who these psychologist types think they are," she'd fumed, slamming the frying pan into the sink. "Them with their fancy diplomas. Anyone with two brain cells to rub together can remember clear as day times before five years of age. Five!"

"Four, Tilly. It's four." Walter regretted the words as soon as they left his mouth, but he pressed on. "The fifth year of life… it means that one is four years old."

She looked at him kindly, but with a hint of impatience, as though he were being obstreperous. Walter waved his hand, brushing his words away.

"Anyways, four," Tilly said doubtfully, before picking up where she left off. "Well, I ask you! I recall sure as anything sitting in the pram one day on the back porch – Ma used to set us babies out there to catch the air – anyways there I was, watching the dogs play with something orange. They were rompin' and barkin' up a storm, chasing each other around the yard. I didn't know what that orange thing was, just that it was a thing and it was orange."

Tilly rinsed the frying pan and hoisted it, dripping, to the stove. Walter eyed the wet spots on the floor, then returned his gaze to Tilly, who had not stopped talking, not noticed the small puddles she'd left by her feet.

"A few years later," she continued, "my sister Doris told me I was too small to remember Ginger the cat, who disappeared around my first birthday. Doris loved that cat, I guess."

Tilly turned to face Walter, her grin revealing a gap in her front teeth. Once again, she'd forgotten to put in her bridge.

"Guess I knew sumpin' Doris didn't. Ha!"

Tilly's laugh barked like a shovel scraping against pavement. It always brings Walter a smile, and the recollection of it now causes his mouth to turn up. Tilly is a blessing to him, not much younger than he, which suits him just fine. The younger, prettier home-care workers he'd had right after the accident made him uncomfortable; he never felt he could relax entirely with them around, and they were usually tight-lipped and economical in their duties. For all she's noisy and opinionated and a terrible cook, Tilly's just fine. In fact, she's perfect.

The egg sits like a stone in his stomach as he settles into his chair to look out the window. A parade of laughing girls passes by on the sidewalk below, school kilts fluttering and arms waving in unselfconscious gestures, newly-long legs gazelle-like, awkward steps taken in clunky shoes. Soon these girls will be accustomed to their full height, their long arms and legs, but for now they are young and gangly, wary of their female-ness.

The weather is fine, a clear late-summer day. The sun bounces off the schoolgirls' ponytails, carrying with it the echo of their voices.

Walter's earliest memory is one of not being listened to. Of this he is certain; the details, however, are revised: memories tangled with imagination equals history. History changes all the time, he knows; it's the prerogative of a story's keeper.

Perhaps when Tilly returns to cook supper he'll resume their conversation about early recollections – hers, if he's honest with himself – Tilly always takes the reins in any conversation. Idly he looks down at the sidewalk.

Walter has made a game of counting the earbuds and mobile devices in use, especially during the busy pedestrian times of day. Of those walking alone, more than half are engrossed in small bits of machinery, wires travelling from ears to pockets, cell phones and BlackBerrys stuck to the sides of heads. Sometimes not; there are those who sport cyborg-like ear devices and walk down the street with their arms swinging, unencumbered, talking in voices louder than regular conversation. Not so long ago, such people were cause for alarm. Now they're given a respectful and uninterrupted berth.

They are as cut off from the world as Walter, only voluntarily so. Just such a man is heading for the intersection, overtaking pedestrians with long, purposeful strides, his trench coat flapping. With his left hand he holds a mobile to his head; his jaw is working animatedly. His approach to the changing light is too fast, his right hand before his face as he looks at his watch. Walter stops breathing as the familiar thudding fills his ears.

Slow down, you...

The light changes from green to yellow, to red, and Walter's face flushes hot, the top of his head tingling.

Stop, for god's sake, stop...

The man is still talking, still looking at his watch, not yet conscious of this street scene. He has not seen the light's change, is unaware of moving traffic.

Watch out!

His left foot reaches the curb as a car races towards him through the intersection.

And then he stops.

There is no slamming of brakes and no sickening thud; no whump-hiss of air-bags deploying; no chemical stench to fill the throat as the adrenaline kicks in. There is nothing.

Walter blows out and then sucks in a burning gulp of air, once, twice, as though surfacing from too long under water. Deliberately he slows his breathing, buries the panic deep in his lungs, his legs, his trembling feet.

At times like this the taste of death sits cold on his tongue.

The man nods twice, then flips the mobile shut, tucks it away in his pocket. He looks left, then right, and then he crosses the now-empty street against the red light.

Walter sits back and fishes around his pocket for a handkerchief. Slowly he pats the sweat from his forehead, reaches for the water glass Tilly has left on the table at his side. It is safe to breathe now.

A pigeon lands on the windowsill, unaware that it is being watched from less than a foot away. Rather than tap the glass, Walter looks at it. The bird is hefty, bobbing around on its dirty orange feet, toes pointed inward. But there is a certain beauty, Walter decides, as the sunlight plays with the feathers, the oily blue-green shimmering opalescent as the pigeon's neck pulses in quick moves, hopeless gestures as it pecks around for food that is not there. The bobbing slows to a gentle bow; the bird pauses and turns its head, affording Walter a close look at one perfect, shining eye, a tiny orange orb that hints at a personality.

The telephone rings from a distance. Walter looks away for a moment while he thinks where he's left it: on the kitchen counter, too far for him to struggle out there before the ringing stops. When he looks back at the window, the pigeon is gone.

Walter frowns, surprised at the depth of his disappointment at the departure of the pigeon. *Damned winged vermin*, Tilly calls them. She is forever galled by the audacity of the birds, and scrubs the windowsill with a ferocity that far exceeds the need. Walter glances at the windowsill and smiles faintly at the sight of the white smear left by his avian visitor.

There is comfort in the clattering of pots, in Tilly's vocalizing while she cooks, even in her off-key humming along with the easy-listening radio station. She keeps the radio's volume down at his request, but her own sporadic blasts puncture the relative quiet when she remembers the words, as though someone were turning a dial in and out of range.

You light up my life...

In spite of himself Walter fills in the words, long-remembered from hateful school dances, those forced embraces on the gymnasium floor with various girls he'd pretended to want. Finally the song ends, its final cadence ending on a dramatic and wobbly note, a Linda Ronstadt special. That he remembers the song and the songstress is no surprise to Walter. His perfect memory, a useful tool in his professional life as an historian, is more often these long and empty days an irritant. Walter shakes his head as though to clear out the insipid melody.

"What's for supper, Tilly," he calls out.

"Spaghetti," Tilly hollers back at him. "And sumpin' special."

Spaghetti means overcooked noodles drenched in canned tomato sauce. Maybe this time he'll get to it before she empties half the canister of Parmesan cheese on it. *Sumpin' special* could mean anything. Walter can't resist asking.

"Specialty of the day, is it?"

"It's a surprise. I grew it myself, right healthy. Wait and see."

He waits. And when the time comes, he sees. Noodles sit wetly in a pool of red sauce. Alongside the pile of pasta something green and stringy slumps on the plate.

"Ah, spinach, is it?"

"Nope. Guess again." Tilly folds her arms and watches him expectantly. Walter hooks a green strand on the tines of his fork and brings it to his mouth. It is bitter, tough against his teeth, and at the same time mushy, like stewed Kleenex. He chews a while, gives up, and swallows, chasing it down with a gulp of water.

"Swiss chard?"

Tilly frowns. "Everyone knows a char's a kind of fish, if you don't mind my saying. Don't know about the Swiss kind, but my brother Billy says the Arctic char ain't what it used to be, and he oughta know, been fishing nearly forty years. No, not Swiss char. Give up?"

Walter nods and hides his upturning mouth behind his napkin. He sucks at a gristly strand caught in his teeth.

"Okay, I'll tell you, then. Dandelions. Them's dandelions."

Walter stops sucking, stares at the pile of green on his plate. Looks up at Tilly's broad face, now split by a toad-like grin. Thankfully, wherever she's been this afternoon, she's found her teeth.

"Yep, dandelions. I picked 'em myself this morning. Why let a perfectly good thing go to waste? I mean, there it was, growing like crazy in the yard. So I picked it."

Walter wipes his mouth, chooses his words carefully.

"Tilly, you don't have a dog, do you?"

"A dog? No, we hadda' put old Major down last winter after he ate the neighbour's garbage. Musta' got some glass in him, the vet figured, all the blood he was passing. A dog, nope. Why d'you ask?"

"No reason, really. So tell me, um… dandelions." Walter can't wait to hear Tilly's pronouncement on dandelions.

"It's right healthy, you know. Makes your bones strong."

"Oh?"

"Yep, it's the milk does it."

"Sorry, what… milk?"

"Sure." Tilly lowers her head as though he were being particularly obtuse. "You know when you pick 'em, that white stuff that gums up your hands. Milk."

"Dandelion milk?"

"You eat up, there, Perfessor. It's good for what ails ya."

There is nowhere to hide the wilted dandelions, no dog to feed under the table, no way of reaching the compost bin under the sink without her seeing. So Walter plods through the meal and thinks ahead to the Mozart piano concerto that will be his reward later in the evening.

Tilly is good for what ails him. And what ails him is no longer physical, now that the casts have come off and the physiotherapists have done their work. The psychiatrist hasn't been able to talk him out of his worries, and Tilly doesn't bother to try to persuade him out the door. What she gives him is an escape from his losses, his memories. What she does is talk him out of himself.

Walter knows well enough that starting a conversation with Tilly is akin to jumping onto a runaway horse. There's no guessing where they'll wind up, but it's a welcome change from the structure of his previous life: the predictable conversations with colleagues; the years of his lectures on art history; even the pillow-talk he once shared with Jeremy.

Tilly counts out his pills, puts them in the Dixie cup, and hands them to him.

"Best take 'em now, I gotta leave a few minutes early tonight. I'm picking up Doris for Bingo."

"Doris?"

"My sister, Doris. Her car's just back from the shop – her youngest had a fender-bender coming off the bridge."

Walter freezes, holding the pills just before his mouth. A sudden prickle of sweat forms above his lip.

"A fender-bender?" he asks.

"God love him, he's okay," Tilly chuckles, "but the tail light sure wasn't, that and the bumper. My jeeze, it'll take him a little while to pay it off, though." Tilly shakes her head, smiling. "He's a good kid, just learned to drive."

Walter suppresses a shudder.

"But my sister, Doris, she's angry as a bag of hornets just now, don't want no one driving it at night, not even herself."

"The same sister who loved the orange cat?" Walter knocks back the pills and wipes the sweat from his lip. Holds out the empty cup.

"That's the one," Tilly grins as she checks the cup. "You've got a mind like a steel trap, there, Perfessor. Me, I've got a memory like a sieve – can't tell you what I had for breakfast, even. What's your earliest memory, anyways? You never did tell."

As if she'd given him the chance. Walter presses his fingertips together, waiting to see if she'll jump in before he starts. In a moment of rare stillness, she is actually looking at him, her eyes expectant.

"I remember sitting in a high chair," he says slowly. "The tray was sort of red melamine shot with black, an imitation marble."

"We had one just like it, only green. I remember my baby brother Billy sitting in it, throwing his beans around for the dogs to eat. Go on."

"Perhaps you'll remember it had a metal rim to keep the food from spilling on the floor."

"Yep." Tilly is nodding vigorously. "Yep, I remember it. Fat lot of good it did, though, but anyways. Go on."

"Well, as I recall there was a square of toast, or perhaps it was cut into fingers. That part isn't clear in my mind, but the sight of scrambled eggs spread about before me is. I was picking up bits of egg in my fist and cramming it in my mouth."

"Kinda like you do here at breakfast, eh? Ha!"

Walter smiles at the pleasant jolt of her laugh.

"Kind of, yes," he says.

"Well, I gotta go," Tilly says. The legs of her chair cough across the floor as she stands. "Doris hates being late for the first call. She's gotta set up her daubers just right, then line up her three beer so she don't have to get up and miss anything. I won't hear the end of it if I'm late. See you tomorrow."

"See you tomorrow, Tilly."

The silence in the apartment is unbearable. Walter picks up the remote and soon the air is filled with Mozart, a close second to Tilly's booming chatter.

He sits back and closes his eyes, puts himself in the long-ago high chair. His mother, with her wavy brown hair (perhaps a memory added later after seeing photographs of her as a young woman) was busy washing dishes. Walter was busy with his scrambled egg.

And then he had something to say.

He spoke to his mother, of what he can't recall, and won't allow his imagination to invent. What he does recall is his mother's laughter.

"Aren't you cute," she'd said.

This was not the reply he'd expected, so he spoke again. Again she laughed, and she told him he was a funny little thing. Walter remembers kicking his feet against the foot rest, the clang of his baby shoes against metal.

Again, he told her something.

Again, she didn't listen.

Walter picked up the toast and threw it on the floor.

Walter opens his eyes. The Mozart has stopped playing. In the silence, the remote lies on the floor in pieces.

The view from the window on Saturdays is always interesting. There are no lulls in foot traffic, as there are on weekdays during work and school hours, and it's with a different sort of purpose that people carry themselves.

Early this morning Walter counted seven nurses leaving the hospital nearby, three of them standing at the bus stop in sensible shoes, chatting and nodding, some of them rubbing their eyes after a long night shift. It's a clear day, which means the oldies will be out later this afternoon for the free concert in the park. Walter imagines the gazebo with its red roof, well-intended cymbal crashes drowning out the rest of the band as white heads nod in rhythm from their seats on park benches. Later on Walter will have Tilly close the window so he may rest to the strains of Vivaldi, or perhaps Ravel.

Of course he'll need to turn on the CD manually. He won't say anything to Tilly about the broken remote, which is wrapped in plastic at the bottom of the garbage chute, his first solo foray from the apartment to the disposal down the hall; how he managed it in his own time, alone, with a minimum of worry and only one breathless grab at the opened door. All of this he will keep to himself.

For now he is content to watch a trio of young mothers marching energetically along the other side of the street, each of them sporting a small baby dangling from a harness tied around the women's fronts. They are smiling, the mothers, at a shared joke. Head bands hold the hair back from their faces so he can see the exchange happen, the sudden surprise of the punch line followed by hands to a mouth, a head thrown back in delight. Delicate fingers find babies' middles, their soft cheeks and chins, unconscious maternal reaches as the women resume their stride.

Walter is grateful for the view from his window, whether it be young mothers laughing or a pigeon resting on the ledge. The window vignettes enrich his thoughts and push his sorrows deep inside, safely out of the way until darkness falls.

Tilly is late. Walter frowns as he looks at the clock. Slowly he makes his way to the kitchen and flicks off the coffee maker and dumps the dregs from his cup. He casts a look at the newspaper, which he has folded, as always, as though he has not read it. Today there is a story about a man who married a woman who has had a partial sex change, and changed her name from Martha to Martin. Martin will be able to bear the happy couple's children, but not breast-feed them. Walter is curious to know what Tilly thinks of this.

But she is not here, has not called to explain her tardiness.

Walter picks up the paper and skims through it, pausing at a headline espousing of all things the health benefits of dandelion greens. He breathes a short laugh – Tilly was right about the bloody dandelions – and moves on to the crossword puzzle, feeling for his pen, still a fixture in his shirt pocket even after all these months away from teaching. It's difficult to break even the most mundane habits, but the convenience of the pen in his pocket gives Walter a small measure of satisfaction as he sits at the kitchen table and begins to solve the puzzle. He works at it until the sound of the key in the door catches his ear. Rather than acknowledge, Walter chooses to ignore Tilly's arrival. She enters the kitchen without a word, looks at him, then moves to the refrigerator and opens the door.

"'Morning, Tilly," Walter finishes the last word of the puzzle, *vesper*. He looks up to see her square back to him, her hand on the open door.

"Late start today?" he asks.

She gives a slight nod, then reaches in for juice, bread, eggs. Walter frowns at her unresponsiveness.

"Have you seen today's paper?"

"No," she says. Her voice is quiet, hoarse. Now that she is facing him, Walter sees that her eyes are bloodshot, her features heightened by deep grooves around her mouth, between her eyebrows. Until now, he's never noticed the knob at the end of her nose, but today it is shiny with pronounced veins.

"Rough night at the Bingo hall?" he asks. Tilly shakes her head slowly, and her hand travels to the side of her head.

Hungover, she looks hungover, he thinks. He might as well be direct.

"Tilly, have you been drinking?"

Her blue eyes snap into focus. The skin around her mouth is white, her lips a thin, straight line.

"Beg pardon?" Her words are clipped as though amputated.

"You seem out of sorts, is all. And you're quite late, if you don't mind my saying."

"I don't mind you keeping your damned trap shut, is what I don't mind."

Walter fixes a hard stare on her.

"I will not be spoken to in this manner, not by anyone but especially not by you."

His words erupt, Vesuvius-like, and land hard. Tilly's blank eyes widen then narrow, then her gaze falls to the floor. The slump of her shoulders is practically audible. Breathing slowly, Walter rises from the table and limps toward the living room.

"I'd like just toast this morning, Tilly. Jam. No eggs. I've already had my coffee."

The toast she brings him is burnt. Jam drips off the edges onto his trousers. He never does find out what she thinks of Martha/Martin, and by the end of the day they have exchanged no more than six words, each of them monosyllables. As she is putting on her coat, Walter looks up from his book.

"You were right about the dandelions," he says, patting the folded newspaper on the table beside him. "They're good for what ails you."

She refuses his verbal offering, granting him only a passing glance as she pulls on her jacket.

"I hope you'll be in better spirits on Monday, Tilly."

By the look she gives him, even before she speaks, he knows she will not be back on Monday. There is a slow revving of his heart, tightness in back of his throat as she forms the words he cannot bear to hear.

In a quiet made quieter by Tilly's absence, even under the cover of Gould's early *Goldberg Variations*, Walter sets the kitchen table, places a linen napkin beside the plate of lightly scrambled eggs. He unfolds the newspaper and brings a fork full of egg to his mouth, and reads the headline: "Cell Phone Accident Claims Teen." A young man has killed himself, texting while driving. His passenger, a teenage girl, survived.

Walter knows that somewhere, in a hospital room, the girl lies bound by guilt and plaster, attached to the living by a series of tubes and wires. He wonders if she will also greet her days by staring at an empty pillow.

The dead boy's aunt is quoted, *He's a good kid, just learned to drive.*

Walter thinks of Tilly's square face split by a grin; of the boy's mother, angry as a bag of hornets.

He sets the fork down on the plate, the egg now gone cold.

A Certain Grace: Five Miniatures

1. Cherry Pits

I was a little girl when my grandfather died. I loved him well enough, but I was also a little scared of him. Grampie had eyebrows like brooms and a laugh like a foghorn, and when Ma took me and Jimmy for a visit, he'd pretend to pull peppermints out of our ears. We thought it was magic until one time his hand was shaking so bad he dropped Jimmy's before he could pull it out of his ear. From then on we knew how he done it. But he never done it again.

Grampie always said he had the biggest nose on the Island. You couldn't help but stare; it was as big as the blade of a shovel, and right under it was his moustache, which was as crazy as his eyebrows. So his face was mostly all nose and hair.

Ma was with him the day he died. She poured him his tea, black as tar and scalding hot to burn as he liked it. He'd just taken his first sip when his eyes nearly popped out of his head, right under those eyebrows and on either side of that big nose. Ma was sure he'd burnt his tongue, and was after askin' if he wanted some milk when he turned in his seat as though to get up from the table. Instead he leaned forward and landed onto his head, and there he sat with his head on the floor and his arse on the chair. He never did get up. Ma took a full minute before she realized he was dead.

We waked him the next day, and the house was full of people. Buddy tuned his fiddle, and Uncle Roy got out the spoons and they all just about took the floor out of the kitchen. Jimmy and I got bored, so Ma handed us each a coffee can and told us to go fill it with cherry pits, they were messing up the yard and besides, she'd give us a penny a can. But the picking took too long, so we went into the parlour and pretended to be pious children so we could look at Grampie.

Well, I was only seven and quite short. All I could see was the straight line along the side of the casket, and near to one end of it, shaped like the blade of a shovel was Grampie's nose. And that's all I could see of him. We stood at the foot of the casket and looked up Grampie's nose. His moustache was waxed flat, and you could see right up inside, dark as two caves. Jimmy told me *shh*, and he lined up his cherry pits along the foot of the casket. We took turns flicking. Twice Jimmy flicked cherry pits right up inside of Grampie's nose, and they disappeared forever. Then I flicked one that got stuck in his left eyebrow. Before we could do anything about it, Ma hauled us out back and gave us a thrashing, but I'm sure no one could hear us yelling, they were all laughing so hard. 'Specially Grampie in heaven.

2. *Hairbrush*

Grampie was a naughty little boy. He'd been spoiled senseless as a baby, dressed in frills and fat as a pudding, his arms in folds and those blue eyes of his lost in his cheeks. His mother was vain about his curls, which she might never have cut until one day Grampie's father got sick of pulling brambles out of them and trying to get the knots out with his wooden hairbrush, the child screaming fit to burst, so he took his wife's pinking shears and cut them all away. By then Grampie was too old for frills, and was wearing long pants and suspenders. But still his mother cried and cried over the pile of yellow curls on the floor, so she swept them up and made a little wreath. I still have it; it's the colour of a dead mouse.

The circus was passing through, staying one night in our little town before moving on to the next. Grampie wanted nothing more than to see the circus, but where he'd been naughty the day before, he wasn't allowed. His mother wasn't too pleased about how he'd let the dog into the hen house just to see what would happen, so she told him he had to stay in his room that day. Well, Grampie wouldn't have any of it, so he pulled out the twelve cents he'd hidden under his Bible, and when his mother was busy with the wringer wash, he sneaked out the back door and ran down the street to find the circus. He was running so fast he slipped on a cow pat. I reckon he didn't notice it was on the back of his short pants, or maybe he just didn't care; he was so excited about seeing the circus he just picked himself up and kept running.

Grampie spent an afternoon in heaven, to hear him tell it. He saw a woman doing a handstand on a pony as it trotted around the ring, and a scrawny bear dancing on an upended bucket, only it was more a turning-around bear than a dancing bear. There was a tightrope walker who balanced plates on a stick, and a woman with a beard longer than Reverend MacMillan's, and his was plenty long: it covered his shirt buttons and smelled of tobacco and buttermilk. Anyway, Grampie bought himself some popcorn and a taffy apple, and when he began to feel sick he went home.

It's too bad he hadn't thought ahead, because there on the porch, madder than a hornet, was his mother. She marched him upstairs and pulled down his pat-covered short pants and spanked him so hard with his father's wooden hairbrush, she broke it. And when her husband came home from work a while later and she told him what Grampie'd done, he flew into a fury. Only it wasn't the naughty little boy with the sore bottom he was angry about, it was his broken hairbrush.

3. Grampie's Maps

As a young girl I sometimes wondered about the maps on Grampie's hands. That's what I took them for, maps. Like the one at school, with jagged edges and smooth, only Grampie's maps were brown, and not pink like Canada.

Mother once told me about them.

Grampie'd finally returned to the Island after some years spent riding freight trains to nowhere and everywhere. He was tired of being cold and hungry, and thought he'd spend the winter Home. Everyone said he'd be back on the trains as soon as the thaw came, but in the meantime he took work tending the graveyard.

By this time Reverend MacMillan was ancient and a widower, and he'd hired to keep house an orphan girl who'd been raised by the nuns. Tess needed respectable work, and there's nothing more respectable than being employed by the clergy. She was tall and sturdy, and could split and stack a cord of wood in less time than it took the Reverend to deliver his sermon. She'd done well by the nuns and could recite the Psalms by memory, and she was given to launching into the Lord's Prayer at the drop of a hat. Only problem with Tess, she was always in a rush, which sometimes made her clumsy. More than once she tripped on her skirts while bringing in the eggs, or serving the Reverend his supper.

It was Easter and there'd been a funeral, cranky old Miss Boudreau who'd died of an apolepsy. Grampie was tired and his hands raw from chopping a hole in the frozen ground, which was a lot warmer than the spinster's bed she'd left behind, he'd later tell.

After the service there was sympathy for his blistered hands and talk of him jumping the next train ahead of the thaw, but all Grampie could think of was his supper. The Reverend insisted he dine with him, and instructed Tess to put on an extra potato. Grampie did his best to clean up, although his overalls were filthy from digging. Nothing could be done about it, and good man that he was, the Reverend pretended not to notice.

Perhaps Tess was perturbed by having to put on that extra potato, or maybe she was just nervous having another man in the house. Anyway, she slammed pots and rushed around the kitchen dropping things. Grampie and the Reverend were looking at each other, wondering what they might talk about, when there was a scream. Like a shot Grampie was in the kitchen, and he threw Tess onto the floor and rolled her up in the carpet. Tess' flaming skirts were doused, but not Grampie; no sooner did he unroll her then she plunged his bubbling hands in the basin, all the while reciting the Lord's Prayer.

Grampie never did ride the freight trains again. I used to sit on his knee and trace the maps, wondering where he might have gone had he not married Tess after the thaw.

4. Gramma's Throne

My grandmother used a toilet seat elevator to help her get on and off the pot. We called it Gramma's throne.

She was a tall woman with white hair pulled back in a little round bun that was covered in a beaded net, and she was given to making stern speeches about good manners. I was a restless girl, and had a hard time not to bounce on her bed. "We must sit like a lady," she'd say, sitting primly with her ankles crossed and her great hands folded. I imagined her doing her business on the throne sitting like a lady. It wouldn't be easy.

Sometimes I was scared of Gramma, like the time she scolded me for resting my elbows on the table. "Young ladies mustn't slouch at the supper table," she said. I wondered why no one scolded her for slouching her neck the way she did, and when later I asked Ma, she told me it was like that because of her widow's hump. But I remembered it from before Grampie had passed and left her a widow. I wondered about that hump.

One time Ma and I went over to Gramma's for a Sunday visit. A nurse was in the bathroom making tut-tut noises and cleaning the floor while Gramma sat at her chair, legs crossed at the ankles and her hands folded. Her lips were pushed together so hard, the wrinkles looked like a spiked flower all around her mouth. The nurse came out of the bathroom and whispered to Ma, and then she left the room. Ma looked at Gramma and Gramma wouldn't look at Ma.

"Mother, what's happened to your throne? The nurse says it's gone."

The spikes around Gramma's mouth got bigger. "It's nobody's business," she said.

"Mother, you need that throne! What have you done with it?"

"I've loaned it to someone who needs it more than I do, and that's all I have to say about it."

If her ankles had crossed any harder, I imagine they'd have snapped. Ma said something about going down the hall to look for Gramma's throne. I was alone with Gramma, sitting on the edge of her bed and trying to cross my swinging ankles without toppling over, worrying that I would do something wrong she'd have to scold me for. Instead she moved her eyes over to me, and her mouth softened.

"Mr. Walters downstairs has it," she said in her scratchy voice. "His balls would sit in the cold water, and so he asked to try it. He finds this much nicer." And then she put a knobby finger to her lips.

That night I took two of Ma's tennis balls and put them in the cold water in the toilet. I wasn't sure how Gramma's throne would make it any nicer, but it was the only time she had ever told me a secret, and it made me feel special.

5. Last Dance

The first time Grampie took Tess to a barn dance was also the last.

Grampie'd scrubbed his one pair of overalls in the trough out back, and hung them to dry 'til they were stiff from the sun and the salt air. He hated them starchy clean, and knew as he was dressing that he'd have a rash on his thighs by the time the evening was over. Still, he clipped the straps into place and knotted a grimy kerchief to cover the burnt skin of his neck. Then he slicked back his hair and tamed his eyebrows using the bacon fat he kept in a tin cup.

Grandma Tess was a great beauty, to hear him tell it, with flaming hair and wild, blue eyes, neither of which the nuns had been able to tame. She was tall and strong and had large, capable hands, and when she walked, her heels punched the earth with a certain grace. Grampie was sure she would fly across the dance floor.

They walked the four miles under a purple sky to the Boutiliers' barn, Grampie's legs held apart so as not to rub them raw, and Grandma Tess swinging her great hands, her heels driving into the dirt road. Neither of them spoke; neither looked to the left nor the right.

When they arrived the dancing was under way. Buddy's fiddle soared over his wife Alice's hammering of the keys, and strong voices carried the tunes through the air. Taken by the sound of the strathspey, Grampie took Tess' large hand into his own, and drug her to the floor, where he whirled her around with solemnity. Before long his face was streaming with sweat and bacon fat, drenching his neckerchief. When a lament slowed them, his idea of dancing cheek-to-cheek was to dance head-to-head, like goats. Luckily for him, Tess was a tall girl.

Soon came a jig, followed by a reel, by which time Tess had shed any shyness the nuns might have instilled. She whirled and stomped, and more than once neighbouring dancers had to duck to avoid her hands, which flew at them like large birds. Finally she stepped too close to a rotting floorboard and put her heel through it, and a nail drove right into her foot.

Grampie half-carried her home the four miles, through a sudden storm in a dark made darker by the flash of pink lightning blown in from the sea. By the time he helped Tess through the kitchen door, his thighs were numb with rash. He knew the sting would keep him awake for nights to come, but when Tess put her hand to his heart it didn't matter.

Acknowledgements

Many pairs of eyes passed through these stories in their early stages; for this I am deeply grateful, most particularly to my Writers' Circle, Carol Bruneau, MG Vassanji, and Mary Lou Payzant.

For his time, insight, and friendship, much gratitude to John Calabro, my editor at Quattro Books.

I am indebted to Parker Duchemin, Edward Fenner, and Allan Briesmaster for their belief in this work; also to Geoffrey and Mary Lou Payzant, Jim Hopkins, and John Drisdelle for their gifts of story.

"A While Ago" is for my brothers.

The Elizabeth Bishop Society of Nova Scotia provided invaluable time and space to write during my two residencies (2010 and 2011) at the Elizabeth Bishop House in Great Village, NS.

My sincere thanks to the Nova Scotia Department of Communities, Culture, and Heritage for providing support during the writing of *A Certain Grace*. My thanks also to the literary journals that first printed several of these stories: *Existere Journal of Arts and Literature* ("A While Ago"), *All Rights Reserved* ("Cherry Pits"), *Glossolalia* ("Gramma's Throne"), and *The Adirondack Review* ("Scars," previously titled "Absolution").

Gratitude to my husband, Tim, whose support and understanding exceed all reasonable bounds.

Many thanks to Quattro Books for taking a chance on short stories.

QUATTRO NOVELLAS

The Ballad of Martin B. by Michael Mirolla
Mahler's Lament by Deborah Kirshner
Surrender by Peter Learn
Constance, Across by Richard Cumyn
In the Mind's Eye by Barbara Ponomareff
The Panic Button by Koom Kankesan
Shrinking Violets by Heidi Greco
Grace by Vanessa Smith
Break Me by Tom Reynolds
Retina Green by Reinhard Filter
Gaze by Keith Cadieux
Tobacco Wars by Paul Seesequasis
The Sea by Amela Marin
Real Gone by Jim Christy
A Gardener on the Moon by Carole Giangrande
Good Evening, Central Laundromat by Jason Heroux
Of All the Ways To Die by Brenda Niskala
The Cousin by John Calabro
Harbour View by Binnie Brennan
The Extraordinary Event of Pia H. by Nicola Vulpe
A Pleasant Vertigo by Egidio Coccimiglio
Wit in Love by Sky Gilbert
The Adventures of Micah Mushmelon by Michael Wex
Room Tone by Gale Zoë Garnett